"Being Able To Love Is A Talent . . . Like Playing The Piano,"

he said wryly. "Some people have it, and some people don't. I don't."

"You can achieve anything if you want it badly enough," she reminded him. "Isn't that what you used to teach me?"

"You know what they say," Jason tossed back with a twisted smile. "Those who can, do. Those who can't, teach."

Lauren was shocked by the utter futility in Jason's voice. She suddenly knew the reason why, as a young girl, she'd found his eyes so scary: a kind of despair of ever being loved darkened them. She longed to reach out to him, to tell him how much she'd always loved him, but she knew he would only react sarcastically. She was also beginning to realize how much pain was buried behind his sardonic facade. She wondered who had hurt him so deeply that he refused to let himself love again.

And suddenly, she had to know.

Dear Reader,

Welcome to Silhouette! Our goal is to give you hours of unbeatable reading pleasure, and we hope you'll enjoy each month's six new Silhouette Desires. These sensual, provocative love stories are both believable and compelling—sometimes they're poignant, sometimes humorous, but always enjoyable.

Indulge yourself. Experience all the passion and excitement of falling in love along with our heroine as she meets the irresistible man of her dreams and together they overcome all obstacles in the path to a happy ending.

If this is your first Desire, I hope it'll be the first of many. If you're already a Silhouette Desire reader, thanks for your support! Look for some of your favorite authors in the coming months: Stephanie James, Diana Palmer, Dixie Browning, Ann Major and Doreen Owens Malek, to name just a few.

Happy reading!

Isabel Swift
Senior Editor

SDRL-7/85

GINA CAIMI
Unfinished Rhapsody

Silhouette Desire

Published by Silhouette Books New York

America's Publisher of Contemporary Romance

SILHOUETTE BOOKS
300 E. 42nd St., New York, N.Y. 10017

ISBN: 0-373-05270-7

First Silhouette Books printing March 1986

America's Publisher of Contemporary Romance

Printed in the U.S.A.

Books by Gina Caimi

GINA CAIMI

started making up her own fairy tales when she was six years old. It was the only way she could get through arithmetic class. She sculpts as a hobby, adores the opera, ballet and old movies but writing remains her major passion. And she still hates arithmetic.

One

Lauren Welles stood transfixed in the doorway as she surveyed the room she thought she'd never see again. Tears misted her pale-green eyes, giving them the limpid translucency of the ocean whose pounding roar she could hear through the closed windows. With long, delicate fingers, she clutched the two suitcases she was carrying as if they contained all that she had left in the world.

Little Orphan Annie! She managed a self-mocking smile, but was unable to hold back a feeling of deep, aching loss. It swept over her, taking her back in time...

She was thirteen years old again, standing in the same doorway, her schoolbag, filled with her precious sheet music, clutched to her skinny body. She was a shy, awkward child, with huge eyes in a thin, too serious little face. Newly orphaned, frightened but dry-eyed, she surveyed what the tall, dark stranger named Jason Caldwell had just told her was to be her new home.

Lauren had never had a home, at least not in the conventional sense, because her mother and father had traveled constantly. She'd been raised mainly by nannies until she turned five; then she was placed in an exclusive boarding school. Her parents' Park Avenue duplex, which she visited only on holidays and vacations, had seemed more like an enchanted palace than a home to her. Just as Laura and Steven Welles had been far too extraordinary to be anything so mundane as parents. One thing was certain—no other girl in school could boast a mother or father with such beauty and glamour.

Lauren adored them and lived only for their visits. The gaiety and excitement they brought to everything they did together lingered in her memory long afterward, brightening the endless gray days in school. Now that they were gone, her life would be all gray days; no sudden bursts of color would make them bearable.

Even in death, Lauren's parents retained the glamour and mystery that had made them both unique. For three days, the newspapers headlined the story of the disappearance of their yacht during an off-season storm in the Caribbean. Detailed accounts and pictures of Laura and Steven Welles's fun-filled escapades and extravagant society balls took up pages of print. When their bodies were found, front-page photos showed the "fairy-tale couple" as Lauren would always remember them: glamorous, carefree, glowing with the sheer joy of being alive.

The fact that a child had survived their union was reported as a postscript; she had been made the ward of Jason Caldwell.

Jason Caldwell was the scariest man she'd ever met; Lauren was sure of it as she clutched her schoolbag even tighter to her chest. Didn't he know it was rude to stare? *She* knew that, and she was only thirteen, while he had to be as old as almost thirty. His eyes were the scariest thing about him. They were the darkest eyes she'd ever seen. Not because of their color, though they were almost black. They were dark deep inside, in a way she couldn't understand, and it frightened her. So he wouldn't see that he had the power to frighten her, Lauren kept her eyes glued to the floor.

"Jason, I don't think she likes it," said the tall, thin lady standing at his side. "I told you we should have put her in the upstairs bedroom." With a fluttery sigh, the woman bent over until her face was level with Lauren's. "Don't you like your new home, dear?"

Lauren looked up into eyes the same startling shade of blue as her mother's, but without her mother's irrepressible glow. "Yes, ma'am," she murmured politely.

"Oh, please don't call me ma'am. It makes me feel so ancient." She laughed. She had a high, girlish laugh, though she was even older than Jason Caldwell, years older. Her skin had the same delicate porcelain tone as Lauren's mother's but had a lot more lines in it, and her hair, which she wore pulled back into a knot, was a faded blond instead of platinum.

Everything about her had a slightly faded quality, Lauren noticed. Except for her eyes, you couldn't say she was pretty, unless you were trying to be polite. But she had a terrific smile. Lauren really liked it. Unlike most grown-ups, her eyes smiled, too, and then it made you feel good just to look at her.

"I'm your Aunt Clarissa," she went on in a chummy manner. "You can call me that...or you can call me Auntie...or just Clarissa. Whichever you prefer."

Lauren had to think about it for a moment. "I like Clarissa best."

Clarissa laughed again, as though she'd found Lauren's solemn answer amusing. "And I will call you Laurie. Lauren's too big a name for such a little girl."

Lauren was about to say that she wasn't a little girl anymore, but she didn't want to seem impolite. She even endured a pat on the head fit for a five-year-old.

"And if you don't like this room, Laurie, just say so, and I'll find you another."

Lauren could tell that Aunt Clarissa was trying very hard to be nice, but she obviously wasn't used to having a child around and wasn't quite sure what to do with one. People who didn't know what to do with children were usually very nice to them, Lauren had noticed.

"For Christ's sake, Clarissa!" Lauren jumped at the unaccustomed sound of a big, booming, masculine voice. "How can the girl tell whether or not she likes the room when she hasn't budged from the doorway?"

Lauren was sure that Jason Caldwell knew what *he'd* like to do with a child—roast it in a slow oven and eat it for Sunday dinner, from the look of him.

"Come on in, Lauren. Don't hang back," he urged gruffly. "Nobody's going to eat you."

Lauren stopped breathing. Could he read minds, too?

"But, Jason," Aunt Clarissa mercifully interceded, "these rooms are too large for the child. The upstairs bedroom is far more suitable."

Jason Caldwell's dark eyes narrowed, making them even scarier, and when he spoke, his voice was as cold as icicles. "I feel very strongly about this, Clarissa. I know the run of the house is your department, but I don't want you to put the girl in that room.''

Aunt Clarissa laughed, a little too gaily. "But why not? That was your room when you were a little boy."

"Exactly." Jason Caldwell smiled, if you could call what was twisting the hard line of his mouth a smile. "I don't want the girl to be shut away in a stifling little room in the furthest wing of the house that used to be the servants' quarters. I want her to feel that she's part of the family, not—" His voice broke off, and he turned away abruptly, leaving Aunt Clarissa looking as surprised as Lauren.

"At least this way she'll have her own bedroom and bath," he continued, pointing toward the arched doorway to a room Lauren couldn't see from where she was standing. "Once she starts school in Provincetown, she'll make new friends, and she can entertain them here in her own parlor." With a sweep of his big arm, he indicated the large, L-shaped room though Lauren could glimpse only part of it. "*She'll* never have to worry about imposing on the adults or being in anybody's way."

"Why, Jason, I never realized you'd felt that way," Aunt Clarissa murmured in a shocked tone of voice. "Why didn't you—"

"Let's see how the girl feels about it," he interrupted. Lauren stiffened as he took a step toward her. "Come on in, Lauren," he insisted gruffly. "This is your home, too, now. You decide whether or not you want to stay in these rooms."

From his tone and manner, Lauren got the feeling that he thought her old enough and clever enough to make up her own mind. For a moment, she almost liked the big, rough man who stood towering over her. She looked up at him, right into his dark, scary eyes. "Yes, sir."

"Sir?" He frowned at her use of the word. Lauren wondered whether she should have called him Uncle Jason, instead. "The girl is too damn polite," he stated bluntly. "What did they do to her in that school?"

No one would ever accuse *him* of being too polite, Lauren thought. She lowered her eyes so he couldn't read her mind.

"Jason!" Aunt Clarissa laughed lightly, but her laugh sounded forced. "The way you talk...in front of the child."

"Child?" He smiled harshly. "Did you see her eyes? Those aren't the eyes of a child."

"She's only thirteen."

"Thirteen going on thirty," he muttered. "All right," he added before Clarissa could protest again. "I'll watch my language."

"See that you do," said Aunt Clarissa sternly; then she smiled at Lauren to show that she was kidding. "These rooms really are lovely, Laurie. Of course, they need to be redecorated; they haven't been used in such a long time." Placing her slender arm around Lauren's shoulders, she drew her away from the door. "We didn't get a chance to fix them up for you because everything happened so—" She caught herself, regret darkening her eyes, and bit down on her bottom lip as if to keep any more words from tumbling out.

"Why don't you and Lauren come up to Boston with me on Tuesday?" Jason Caldwell was quick to offer in his raspy voice. "You can spend the day shopping for new drapes, wallpaper, whatever."

"Oh, won't that be fun, Laurie?" Aunt Clarissa said gaily, but Lauren could see that her eyes were all teary.

"We do so want you to be happy here." Impulsively, she hugged Lauren to her side, startling her. She wasn't used to being hugged. Jason Caldwell saw her flinch. He frowned again.

"The day parlor is at the back of the house," Aunt Clarissa rattled on as she drew Lauren inside, "so you have a lovely view of the ocean. Do you like the ocean?"

"I don't know. I've never seen one," Lauren was forced to admit. "Except in the movies or on TV."

"Well, here's your chance." A fluttery wave of her hand directed Lauren's attention to the far side of the room.

With eager curiosity, Lauren spun around. What she saw made her heart stop, and she gasped.

"It is a lovely view, isn't it?" said Aunt Clarissa proudly. She might have been talking about a prized family possession.

But Lauren hadn't even noticed the huge bay window that looked out over wind-sculptured dunes alive with rippling, sun-bleached beach grass. Nor did she see beyond the steep plunge of dunes to where the ocean's giant waves crashed against the shore, foaming on the sand. Her dazzled eyes, her whole being, were fixed on the vision in front of the bay window.

"You have a piano?" she breathed. The gleaming ebony instrument standing in the center of the alcove encircled by the bay window was larger than life, but she still couldn't believe her eyes. "A concert grand!" Before she realized what she was doing, Lauren pulled away from her aunt and went rushing over to the alcove.

Her heart pounding with excitement, she dropped her schoolbag on the bench. Tentatively, she reached out and touched the grand piano. It didn't disappear. Warmed by the sunlight streaming through the window, the richly burnished wood felt almost alive to the touch. Lauren's fingers tingled as they glided over the keyboard lid; they trembled when they traced the legendary name, Steinway & Sons. Only then did she realize what she was doing, what she had done. Tearing her hand away, she glanced fearfully at Jason Caldwell.

His dark eyes had been watching her every move, but with intense curiosity rather than disapproval. Lauren let out a tiny sigh of relief.

"Do you like the piano?" he asked on his way over to her.

She nodded with a quick gulp.

Stopping directly in front of her, he stared down at her intently. "I understand you play the piano."

"Does she?" Aunt Clarissa chimed in from across the room. "How lovely."

"Will I be allowed to play this one?" Lauren blurted out. She knew she shouldn't be so bold, but she couldn't help herself. "If I promise to be very careful...and not to scratch it or anything?"

A strange smile twisted the corners of Jason Caldwell's hard mouth. Abruptly, he flipped up the fall board, exposing the keyboard. "Pound away."

That was all the encouragement Lauren needed. Quickly, she slid onto the piano bench. Although she was tall for her age, the bench was too high for her, and she had to stretch her gangly legs in order to reach the pedals. Eagerly, she placed her fingers on the gleaming ivories; then she hesitated. She was always very nervous when she had to perform in front of other people; she was at her best when it was just her and the music.

"Who are your favorite composers?" asked Jason Caldwell.

His tone had been casual, but Lauren could see that he was carefully checking her posture, the way she held her arms and placed her fingers on the keys—just as her music teacher used to do, only more critically.

Her fingers started to cramp and her voice was tight when she answered, "Chopin...and Brahms and... Rachmaninoff."

"A romantic," he muttered dryly.

Lauren wasn't sure exactly what a romantic was. He'd made it sound like an insult. Well, if loving beautiful music made you a romantic, she decided right then and there she wasn't ashamed to be one. She'd meant to play one of her favorite Chopin nocturnes, but now she didn't dare—not in front of somebody who sneered at romantics. Instead she tried some quick, light scales to get the feel of the instrument and help her fingers relax.

"How long have you been playing, dear?" Aunt Clarissa asked on her way over to the alcove. She stopped under the archway, however, and although she'd spoken to Lauren, she was staring at Jason Caldwell with a worried expression.

"Six years," he tossed over his shoulder without giving Lauren a chance to answer; his tone made it clear he was annoyed by the interruption. "Your music teacher, Miss Hanson," he went on, never taking his eyes off the light but careful movement of her fingers, "tells me that they had to lock up the piano to get you to do your homework. And instead of playing games with the other girls, you used to spend all your recreation periods practicing." His dark, probing eyes shifted abruptly to her face. "Is that true?"

"Uh, yes," Lauren admitted haltingly. He was making her very nervous. She couldn't understand why he was asking her so many questions, and she was afraid that he'd get annoyed at her, too, if she gave him the wrong answers. She concentrated on her playing.

She'd always been able to lose herself in her music, to wrap herself up in the beautiful sounds and make the rest of the world disappear. Her fingers rippled off a fluid glissando. The piano's response made her breath catch.

She let the brilliant tones wash over her, but they were unable to shut out the stronger, more insistent sound of Jason Caldwell's voice. "Miss Hanson seems to think that you have a definite gift for the piano." Stepping behind the bench, he peered over her, his huge shadow spilling across the keyboard. "Do *you* think you have a definite gift for the piano, Lauren?"

Lauren hesitated, confused. "A gift?" she repeated dully.

"Do you think you're any good at playing the piano?"

"I...I don't know."

"You don't know?" He came tearing around the bench, a terrifying scowl on his face. "You want to be a concert pianist, and you don't know if you're any good?"

Lauren's fingers froze on the keys.

"Jason, really!" Aunt Clarissa protested.

"Well, do you think you're any good or don't you?" he snapped contemptuously.

"Yes!" Lauren exploded. "But not as good as I'd like to be!" She jumped up from the bench, ready to run from the room, from what she'd done.

She always tried so hard to be obedient and well be-
haved. She'd never dared talk back, the way many of
the others girls in school had. They used to make fun of
her shyness because she never showed her feelings. But
she had lots of feelings deep inside, so many it scared
her sometimes because, when they did come out, it was
with a kind of explosion she couldn't control.

Ashamed, frightened, Lauren rushed out from behind the piano, but Jason Caldwell stepped quickly in
front of her, blocking her way. She froze, anticipating
the punishment to come. She was sure he'd never let her
play the piano again. He'd probably pack her straight
off to boarding school after what she'd just done.

"That's more like it," Jason Caldwell said. He
smiled—a real smile, not one of his twisted ones. And
his eyes weren't dark and scary anymore. When he
spoke again, his voice was soft and deep, strangely
musical.

"Miss Hanson believes you're a great deal better than
good already. But if you're really serious about becoming a concert pianist, *you* have to believe in your talent, Lauren." Darkness filled his eyes again. "There are
too many people out there just waiting to attack real
talent. If you let them see the slightest weakness or insecurity, they'll tear you apart." Blinking away the
darkness, he brought his big, rough face down to hers.
"Do you understand what I'm trying to tell you?"

"Yes, I . . . I think so."

"I'd like to hear you play one of your favorite pieces.
Would you play for me?"

Lauren's throat tightened, making it impossible for
her to answer. Did this mean he wasn't going to send her
back to boarding school?

"Oh, you must play for Jason, Laurie."

Lauren had forgotten that her Aunt Clarissa was standing under the arched entrance to the alcove. From the expression on Jason Caldwell's face when he straightened up, so had he.

"Jason knows absolutely everything there is to know about playing the piano," she went on enthusiastically as she quickly joined them. "He was a brilliant pianist himself once."

Lauren was unable to hide her amazement: that big, rough man who sneered at romantics, a brilliant pianist? For the first time, she noticed his hands, and she stared at them, fascinated. They didn't fit his body but seemed to have been stuck on by mistake. His fingers were long and slender, surprisingly sensitive for such a grizzly bear of a man. They were the hands of a born pianist, but she couldn't keep from asking him, "Were you really?"

He scowled.

Aunt Clarissa laughed. "Yes, believe it or not. Why, Jason would have been a great concert pianist, but—" The look he shot her shriveled the words right on her tongue.

Without missing a beat, his dark gaze slid back to Lauren. "Will you play for me?"

"Yes, but..." She swallowed quickly. "I have to practice first." He nodded in agreement, obviously pleased with her answer, though she'd expected him to be annoyed by it. "Then it's all right if I...practice on this piano?"

"Of course." *Now* he sounded annoyed. He was a very difficult man to figure out, Lauren decided. He studied her intently for some moments. Lauren could see that he was telling himself to be patient with her, and she could tell that patience didn't come easily to him.

He sighed harshly. "Lauren, you don't have to ask permission to play the piano ever again. Do you understand?" He rested his hand almost reverentially on top of the gleaming instrument. "This is *your* piano now."

Lauren's breath caught, and she gaped up at him. She was sure she hadn't heard him correctly.

"Your Aunt Clarissa and I want you to have it," he assured her. Aunt Clarissa looked as stunned by his announcement as Lauren did. "Consider it a welcome-home present."

"It's...it's mine?" Lauren stammered, almost afraid to believe in such happiness. "Do you really mean it? My very own piano?"

"Your very own piano."

"Oh, thank you!" Lauren cried ecstatically. She couldn't remember ever being so happy. In an explosion of mindless joy and gratitude, she threw herself heedlessly into his arms. "Thank you, Uncle Jason!"

His whole body went rigid—he obviously wasn't used to being hugged, either. "Don't do that," he bit out, pulling roughly away from her. Lauren staggered back several steps, shame and humiliation burning her face. "I'm not your uncle," he added darkly.

"Thank your lucky stars, little girl," a mocking voice cut in from behind them. "Imagine having Jolly Jason here for an uncle."

With varying degrees of surprise, they all turned toward the blond young man who was leaning with charming insolence against the arched entrance. Aunt Clarissa's wan face lit up as though someone had just turned on a light inside her. Jason Caldwell's face darkened.

"You can call *me* uncle anytime." The young man sent Lauren a mischievous grin as he pushed away from the arch with his sneaker-clad foot, leaving a long scuff mark on the antique wallpaper.

"Evan, what a wonderful surprise!" Aunt Clarissa hurried to meet him as he started toward them. "But what on earth are you doing home from school?" Her smile lost some of its brilliance, and one corner of her mouth twitched nervously. "Is everything all right?"

He shrugged off her concern. "Sure, Sis. So this is Laura's little girl," he went on quickly, cutting off her attempt at another question. "It's about time we met." He hunkered down in front of Lauren, putting a considerable strain on his skintight designer jeans. "Hi, I'm Evan. What's your name?"

"Lauren. Lauren Welles," she replied with just a trace of her usual shyness. His manner was so free and easy, his smile so dazzling, a person just had to open up to him.

He couldn't have been more than twenty and was so good-looking he was almost as beautiful as a girl. But his features, very fine and perfectly drawn, were a painful reminder to Lauren of her mother's. Especially his eyes. He had the Caldwell eyes, that startlingly vivid shade of blue; but unlike Aunt Clarissa, his eyes held the same irrepressible sparkle as Lauren's mother's.

"Well," said Evan when he'd finished appraising Lauren, "looks like we've got another beauty in the family. Get a load of those eyes." He put his finger under her chin and tilted her face up so she was forced to look right at him. "I'm a real pushover for green eyes," he teased. "Where did you get those eyes?"

"From . . . my father," Lauren stammered self-consciously. She wasn't used to anyone making such a fuss over her.

"But you've got Laura's . . . your mother's extraordinary hair," he murmured as if to himself.

Lauren had always felt embarrassed about having platinum-blond hair because people were always staring at it, making her feel a bit strange. But the approving look on Evan's face made her feel proud of it now.

"You're going to be a real man-eater when you grow up," said Evan with a sexy little growl. "I can tell." Reaching out, he caressed her pale, silky hair. Lauren's eyes widened in surprise. "Once you fill out a bit." His bright-blue gaze slid down the front of her body, over her softly budding curves. "You're starting to already, I see," he teased, making Lauren blush clear through to her bones.

Jason Caldwell's voice broke in harshly. "What are you doing down from Harvard, Evan?"

Evan's fingers released Lauren's hair to wave mockingly at the older man. "Oh, hi, Jason," he said as if he were only now aware of Jason's presence. He gave Lauren a conspiratorial wink. "I see you've already met Jason the Terrible so—"

"All right, Evan," Jason interrupted, his voice hard and insistent. "What happened this time?"

"Nothing," Evan protested in a tone of outraged innocence. He sounded like a child who was tired of being the one the grown-ups always picked on. With a careless shrug, he straightened up and stood looking down at Lauren. "I just had a little trouble."

"Not again, Evan," Aunt Clarissa scolded mildly, more concerned than angry.

Evan shrugged again and wrinkled up his nose appealingly. "It's no big deal. I'll tell you about it later." He flashed his older sister a smile, and her face reflected its brilliance, a moon to his sun. "But first," he went on cheerfully, ignoring Jason Caldwell's frown, "I want to finish getting acquainted with our foxy little Lauren here." He turned his dazzling smile on Lauren with almost the same result.

Aunt Clarissa shook her head indulgently. "Laurie, this is my—and your mother's—naughty baby brother, Evan."

"Half brother, really," Evan corrected, "which makes me your half uncle. You can call me uncle, if you like, but I'd prefer Evan." He slid a sly, taunting glance in Jason Caldwell's direction. "Now, the reason Jolly Jason over there isn't related to you is because he's your mother's stepbrother."

Lauren wasn't sure what a stepbrother was exactly. "You mean, like in the fairy tales?"

"That's right." Evan threw back his shaggy blond head and roared with laughter. "But you know how in most fairy tales they have a wicked stepmother or stepsisters? Well, in our family, we have a wicked stepbrother."

"Evan!" Aunt Clarissa tried to sound shocked, but she ended up laughing indulgently, unable to escape Evan's infectious high spirits. "Laurie will think you're serious. That's no way to talk about your own brother."

"Half brother, please," Evan insisted with a playful groan. He caught the astonished way Lauren was looking from one man to the other. She'd never seen two brothers who looked less alike in every way. "Hard to believe that we both had the same mother, isn't it?"

Lauren nodded. "It's all very confusing."

"Welcome to the mixed-up Caldwell family," said Evan sardonically.

"Evan, please behave," Aunt Clarissa pleaded with a quick, worried glance at Jason Caldwell. "It's really very simple, Laurie," she went on with a tremulous smile. "Our mother died when Laura and I were barely in our teens, and father remarried. Margot, the lady he married, was also widowed, and she had a little boy—Jason."

"And I," interjected Evan drolly, "am the unfortunate result of that second marriage."

"Father legally adopted Jason later on," Aunt Clarissa continued. "But—" she slid Evan a pointed look "—we have always considered Jason a member of the Caldwell family."

A strange smile twisted Evan Caldwell's face, and for a moment he didn't look handsome at all. But he had a long way to go to match his half brother. Jason Caldwell's rough-featured face was sharper and harder than before, and his eyes were dark and scary again.

Lauren noticed how different he was, not only from Evan but from Clarissa as well. No one would ever take *him* for a Caldwell. The light color of their hair, skin and eyes made his seem all the darker; their delicate bone structure made his look even bigger and rougher.

"But don't let the mere fact that Jason doesn't have a drop of Caldwell blood in his icy veins fool you, little girl," said Evan. His tone was playful but had a needling edge to it. "Jason is the most thorough Caldwell of us all. Probably because he works so hard at it."

Lauren couldn't help wondering why Jason Caldwell wasn't responding to his half brother's obvious taunts. He'd physically removed himself from their circle when Evan had first come over to join them. Now, he was removed in a deeper, more personal way. Lauren could tell because she did the same thing when she felt that she was in the way or people didn't like her.

His deliberate silence and proud, impenetrable manner only goaded Evan. "Anyone would think that Jason was the true male heir of the family." He laughed at the bitter irony of it. "He runs all the Caldwell businesses. He holds all the purse strings. He controls everything and everybody in this house, and—"

"That's enough, Evan," Jason Caldwell finally snapped. The authority in his voice and manner was undeniable and had an instant effect on his half brother.

Evan smiled sheepishly, appealingly. "You see what I mean?"

"Now you really are going too far, Evan," Aunt Clarissa chided. "Sometimes your jokes aren't as funny as you mean them to be. Come." She took him firmly by the arm, the way a concerned mother might. "Let's go to your room and get you settled in before you get into any more trouble."

"Me? Get into trouble?" Evan exclaimed with perfect childlike innocence, a mischievous gleam in his big blue eyes.

His half sister smiled up at him lovingly. "Whatever are we going to do with you?"

Aunt Clarissa hadn't looked or smiled at Jason Caldwell that way, Lauren realized, not once. She suddenly felt sorry for the man with the dark, scary eyes and beautiful hands.

"You better watch out, little girl," Evan called over his shoulder mockingly as he allowed Clarissa to drag him out of the room. "Jason is the angry giant, the big bad wolf, and the bogeyman all rolled into one."

The bitter rage that suddenly glared in Jason Caldwell's eyes and twisted his hard mouth sent a chill through Lauren, and made her wonder whether Evan was right about him after all.

But it was Jason Caldwell who looked in on Lauren later that night, who comforted her when she woke up screaming from a nightmare. And it was Jason Caldwell who played the piano until she was able to fall asleep again. The lovely sound of the Chopin nocturnes floated through the open doorway, filling the dark corners of the room, melting all the dark shadows in her mind, suffusing her dreams with music.

And it was Jason, during all the years that followed, who Lauren would run to whenever she was troubled or needed anything. It was always Jason. . . .

Lauren's fingers tightened painfully around the handles of her suitcases. This was the first time that Jason had ever asked for her help. Knowing how proud he was and how much he hated her now, Lauren knew what it must have cost him. What she didn't know was what it was going to cost her.

Two

Taking a long, steadying breath, Lauren walked into the room. She set the suitcases down in front of the sliding pocket doors that separated the parlor from the bedroom. When she straightened up, an uncontrollable shiver went through her that had nothing to do with the dampness in the air.

The parlor was exactly as she'd left it, stirring up more unwelcome memories and feelings. She felt as if she'd suddenly come face-to-face with everything she'd been running away from for the past four years, everything she'd forced herself to forget.

She'd forgotten how much she loved this room. Until that moment, she hadn't realized how much she'd missed it. Her apartment in an ultramodern New York high rise, with its gleaming high-tech furnishings, suddenly seemed cold and sterile by comparison.

With its twelve-foot ceiling, odd-shaped walls, delicate gingerbread woodwork and fancifully patterned parquet floor, the room retained the look and feel of a Victorian day parlor. In true nineteenth-century tradition, colors and textures were mixed and matched. The dominant tones of mauve and dusty rose were set off by touches of deep burgundy, the fragile translucency of lace and crystal balanced by the sturdy solidity of marble and mahogany.

Small, brocaded Victorian headache bags, filled with potpourri, were still tucked in the corners of the mauve velvet love seat. Satin and antique-lace pillows still lounged on a pair of scroll-arm chairs facing each other across the sea captain's chest that served as a cocktail table. Crocheted antimacassars completed the period mood.

In contrast to Victorian homes of the turn of the century, the furnishings were spare, making the parlor light and airy. The carpet sprawling in front of the marble fireplace echoed the muted pinks of the upholstery fabrics, mixing them with the vivid blue of a summer ocean. The glazed walls were the color of soft parchment, and all the windows were covered with long drifts of lace that filtered the bright light reflecting from the beach.

The alcove, with its two-story-high bay window, was still being used as the music room. At its heart stood the concert grand, gleaming as though it had been polished only moments before.

Lauren felt that familiar pull inside her. She slipped out of her trench coat, dropped it on a chair and hurried over to the precious Steinway. The piano was momentarily forgotten, however, as her attention was caught and held by the vision beyond the bay window.

The man stood on the highest sand dune, watching intently for something or someone. He was too far away for Lauren to make out his features clearly, but she had no trouble recognizing him. Her stomach contracted violently, and she had to fight a feeling of panic, an irrational urge to run from the room, from the house, as far away from Cape Cod as she could get.

No one had the power to affect her that way except Jason Caldwell.

Certainly, no one else she knew would be out on the beach on a blustery, late-March afternoon wearing only a sweater and shorts. Storm clouds swirled threateningly in the slate-gray sky, and the ocean looked swollen with rage as it sent wave after wave to batter the shore relentlessly. An east wind howled through the beach grass, twisting and bending the fine ghost-white strands down to the sand, where patches of snow clung tenaciously to their roots.

With his thick black hair blowing wild in the wind, his sweater ballooning like a sail, Jason never looked more in his element. Hands on hips, feet planted firmly apart, he reminded Lauren of a strong, gnarled oak tree that was somehow impervious to the elements, incapable of bending with the breeze.

Killer, Jason's prize Doberman, suddenly bounded into view, the stick he'd just retrieved clenched in his strong jaws. Man and dog wrestled playfully for possession of the stick. Man won. Rising to his full height of six-foot-three, Jason wound up for another throw. Killer, ears pointed, a front paw poised delicately in midair, quivered in anticipation.

As Lauren watched Jason send the stick whizzing out of view, she was struck by the power of his shoulders and back, the strength of his long, muscular legs.

When she was a child, he'd seemed godlike to her, and she'd worshiped him—though she never completely lost her fear of him when he was in one of his dark moods. Yet at times, he could be like the older brother she'd never had, warm and protective, sometimes loving. Always, he was her fiercely demanding teacher. And, ultimately, her tormentor. But she'd never seen him as a man—until that night—and then only because he had forced her to.

Memories of the last time she saw Jason invaded Lauren's mind, making her shiver again. Because of what had happened between them that night, Lauren knew that now she would always think of Jason as a man. A virile, intensely sensual and cruel man.

As though he were somehow aware of her thoughts, of the intensity of her feelings, Jason turned suddenly and looked up at the house. Lauren jumped back from the window. Face flushed, heart pounding, she hid behind the heavy damask drapes that flanked the transparent lace panel. She felt as guilty as a child caught misbehaving.

Damn him that he could still do that to her, she thought resentfully. Well, it was up to her to see that he didn't. She was no longer that shy, adoring young girl he'd dominated so completely. She was a woman now, her own woman, and an acclaimed concert pianist. All the pain and difficulties she'd lived through since running away from home—from Jason—had matured her beyond her twenty-four years. No man, not even Jason Caldwell, could ever take her hard-won independence away.

Not once in the last four years, she reminded herself proudly, not even at her most desperate, had she run back to Jason for help as he had predicted. The only reason she was there now was because Aunt Clarissa was seriously ill and needed her; that was the only reason Jason had swallowed his monumental pride and called her. But if he thought he was going to go on treating her like before, he was in for one hell of a shock.

Lauren smiled with satisfaction—until she realized she was still cringing behind the drapes. With a disgusted sigh, she turned and walked resolutely away from the window, only to be confronted by more memories.

The gray, misty light, filtering though the lacy panels of the window, illuminated the carefully preserved mementos of her girlhood, catching them in delicate, spidery webs of unreality. Time hung, frozen, in the framed photos Jason had taken of her at different stages of her career. All the gold medals she'd won in piano competitions still gleamed in the cases where he had so proudly displayed them.

Lauren was surprised to find everything exactly as she'd left it. Especially when she knew that Jason had forbidden everyone to so much as mention her name in his presence since that night she'd run away and eloped with Carter. Then why had he kept everything as it used to be?

Lauren paused before a photo commemorating her first professional recital when she was sixteen. She laughed softly to herself. Had she really been that young and naive-looking? She had thought she looked so sophisticated in her first grown-up gown, a ruffled, off-the-shoulder vision in white organdy that clung to the soft, young curves of her breasts and tiny waist, then flared over her hips to fall in swirls and swirls of layered ruffles. God, how she'd loved that gown! She could still remember the look on Jason's face when he first saw her in it. It was a look she'd never seen before.

The recital was a great success, one of the happiest nights of Lauren's life. She played brilliantly, but she could never have done it without Jason. For days, she'd been unable to eat or sleep properly for fear of disappointing him. The applause still thundering in her ears, she rushed backstage to find him. In her excitement, she threw herself mindlessly into his arms as she had countless times before, but this time he didn't return her hug. Instead, she felt his whole body stiffen, and he pulled back.

Knowing how emotionally reserved he could be, Lauren assumed that Jason thought her uncontrolled display of emotion inappropriate in front of the strangers crowding her dressing room. It was months before she realized the sudden, inexplicable change in his feelings for her had started that night.

Gone were the big-brotherly warmth, the roughly tender expressions of affection that had always meant so much to her. The more she tried to please him, to win back his love, the more distant he became. She never found out what she had done to cause that change in him. She only knew that in some strange, indefinable way, she had failed him.

Tears stung Lauren's eyes, ached in her throat. She was amazed and angry to find that the loss of Jason's love could still cause her so much pain. Turning away from the photo and the memories it evoked, Lauren started out of the music room, but she was held back by the sight of the leather-bound scrapbook Jason had always kept on her. She didn't remember it as being that thick.

Drawn in spite of herself, Lauren walked over to the bulging scrapbook propped up on a large brass music stand. Her breath caught when she scanned the page it was opened to: it displayed clippings of her Carnegie Hall recital of less than two weeks ago. With trembling hands, she flipped back through the album. Every major review of her work over the past four years had been meticulously preserved.

Lauren shook her head ruefully. What she'd just discovered only proved what she'd known instinctively since she was sixteen. Jason had never loved her; all he cared about was her talent. Now she understood why he'd kept the music room intact—it was a monument to himself. It served to prove that he, with his Svengali powers, had been the one responsible for turning a talented young girl into a world-class pianist.

Thinking back on it now, Lauren couldn't believe what a fool she'd been, how pathetically hard she'd worked to achieve his aims. In her desperate attempt to please him and make him proud of her, she would practice until her fingers were numb and every muscle in her arms and back ached. Because of him, she'd never known the normal, carefree life of a teenager. Her life had consisted entirely of two things: music and Jason. That would have been enough for her if only he'd loved her.

That startling admission took Lauren totally by surprise.

Jason could never love her, she reminded herself bitterly. And even if he could, she no longer wanted or needed his love. She'd fought too long and too hard to stand on her own two feet. Loving Jason would mean the total loss of herself; he would demand nothing less.

"I don't believe this," Lauren muttered, slamming the scrapbook shut. How could she even consider such a thing?

She was drawn back to the bay window as though confronting the source of her dilemma would help her resolve it. In the swiftly approaching twilight, Jason was a dark silhouette jogging along the edge of the water. Intently, she followed his tall, lithe shape as it weaved in and out of the breaking waves, Killer dancing at his heels.

She was willing to admit that Jason was still the only person she'd ever been able to depend on, the one steady rock in the constantly shifting landscape of her life, but had she forgotten what their relationship had been like those last few years?

Although Jason had no longer treated her with the warmth and affection he once had, he continued to dominate her every waking moment. Not merely satisfied with teaching her how to master the piano, he insisted on teaching her how to dress, how to fix her hair and makeup, how to speak and act in public. He selected the clothes she wore, the books she read, the music she listened to or played.

He seemed determined to make her over to fit some image all his own. For a long time, Lauren tried desperately to be the woman he envisioned, the woman she felt she could never be. Then she gave up. She knew she'd never be able to satisfy him.

Still too much in awe of him, too eager for his approval to rebel openly, Lauren began withdrawing more and more into her music again. Her old shyness and insecurity came back to haunt her. She hadn't felt so utterly alone and unloved since boarding school—though

Jason wouldn't love her, he saw to it that no other man would, either.

Fear shivered through Lauren as she recalled Jason's reaction when she'd told him that Carter wanted to marry her. Her long, sensitive fingers clenched protectively into fists. She didn't want to think about that night. For four years, she'd refused to think about what Jason had done to try to destroy her first romance. Why couldn't she stop thinking about it now?

Three

Long-suppressed images and sensations flooded Lauren's mind, stirring up feelings of pain and humiliation and another, even more disturbing emotion. Her nails, though short by necessity, bit deep into the palms of her hands as she remembered....

"What have you done to your hands?" Jason demanded, cutting her off in midsentence.

"I had nail tips put on . . . for the party." Stretching her hands out, Lauren proudly displayed her newly acquired fingernails. They were as long as she'd always dreamed of wearing them—but couldn't because of the piano—and were painted a flaming red. She laughed and wiggled her fingers playfully. "Aren't they beautiful?"

Jason frowned disapprovingly. The reflection from the desk lamp heightened the strong, dramatic lines of his face, making his hair and eyes gleam as darkly as the

black velvet smoking jacket he wore. Sitting impos-
ingly in his oxblood leather chair behind his carved
ebony desk, he looked like an absolute ruler about to
pass judgment on a disobedient subject.

"They were beautiful the way they were," he said,
pushing aside the report he'd been reading. "They were
the hands of an artist. Now they're the hands of a frivolous, mindless little..." He didn't finish the sentence.
He didn't have to: his meaning couldn't have been
clearer. His frown of disapproval shifted to include her
salon-styled hairdo.

Lauren's hand flew self-consciously to her forties
upsweep. Everyone else had told her that she'd never
looked lovelier or more mature. She managed a carefree gesture with her hand and tilted up her chin defiantly. "It's the latest rage. All the girls are wearing it."

Jason couldn't have been more unimpressed. Placing both hands on the edge of his desk, he leaned back
in his chair to get a full-length view of her.

"And where did you get that dress?" he asked flatly.
His eyes narrowed as they moved over her red silk dress,
taking in the low-cut neckline, the way the draped fabric clung to every curve of her body.

"I...I bought it last week on an impulse."

For a long moment, Jason stared at the softly
rounded curve of Lauren's breasts as he realized that she
wasn't wearing a bra.

His eyes darkened—from anger, she was sure. She'd
never dared to go without a bra before, nor had she ever
bought herself a dress without his approval. She simply refused to go to the party in one of those Little Mary
Sunshine dresses Jason always picked out for her. They
made her look and feel even more immature in front of
Carter and his sophisticated friends. Whether Jason

liked it or not, she was a grown woman now, and she was going to start dressing like one. She only wished she had the courage to tell him so.

Jason cleared his throat roughly, but before he could say anything Lauren jumped in, resuming their original conversation. "Jason, please let me have the car tonight."

"I've already told you no, Lauren." He turned his attention back to the report on his desk as if he considered the matter closed and had no intention of discussing it further.

"Why can't I have the car?" she persisted uncharacteristically. She'd promised herself that this time she was going to stand up to him. "You know what a good driver I am."

"Yes, I know." His proud, almost arrogant tone implied that he should know because he'd taught her. Picking up his gold pen, he scribbled a note in the margin of the page he'd been scanning. "That's not the reason."

"Then what is it?"

He underlined the note he'd just made with several bold, hard slashes. "Your escort is the one who should drive you to the party."

"Carter would have driven me," she assured him, moving close to the desk. "But *he's* the one who's giving the party, and he's got so many last-minute details to take care of, and..." Lauren tried to remember the other reasons Carter had given her, but she couldn't.

"There's no excuse for his behavior," said Jason bluntly. "He should have made the proper arrangements."

"Jason, be reasonable," Lauren implored. "Carter's house is less than a mile from here. I'm perfectly capable of driving less than a mile."

"That's not the point." He looked up at her severely. "Only a man who has no respect for a girl would allow her to drive herself to a party she's going to as his date."

"Carter does re—"

"And if *you* had any respect for *me*," he cut her off again, coldly. "you wouldn't have waited until you were already dressed and ready to leave to tell me that you were going to this party."

"But you've been so busy lately...out of town so much," Lauren stammered. She was never any good at telling lies. The look he fixed on her told her that he didn't believe her feeble excuse anyway. He knew she deliberately hadn't told him because she was afraid he'd forbid her to go. "I...I really didn't think it mattered."

"Everything you do matters to me, Lauren," Jason said, his voice thick with emotion. Her eyes widened in surprise; he quickly lowered his. "After all, I'm the one who's responsible for you," he added, his voice resuming its cool, even tone. "And if *you* don't see to it that your escort treats you with the respect you deserve, then *I* will."

Lauren could feel the anticipation and excitement of going to the party slowly draining out of her. "Jason, please," she pleaded, grabbing on to the edge of the desk. "This party means so much to me." In an attempt to get his attention and to narrow the distance the imposing desk put between them, she leaned over it. "Please don't ruin it for me."

"I'm not trying to ruin it, Lauren." As he glanced up at her, the strong craggy lines of his face stiffened in shock. Only then did Lauren realize that the way she was leaning across the desk afforded him a generous view of her unconfined breasts.

She straightened up immediately; he sat up abruptly in his chair.

"All I'm asking," Jason went on as he concentrated on sliding the pen into its cover, "is that your escort come and pick you up at home so he can meet your family properly, and we can meet him."

So you can give him the third degree and scare him away, you mean, Lauren thought resentfully. But she said, "You already know Carter. He's Evan's best friend."

"Not exactly the highest recommendation of moral character one could hope for," he drawled sarcastically. "I've only seen Carter a few times. I know him mainly by reputation." The gold pen gleamed in the reflection of the desk lamp as Jason twirled it almost angrily between his fingers. "Everyone on the Lower Cape knows Carter's reputation with girls. It's even worse than Evan's."

"That's just petty, jealous gossip," Lauren returned defensively. "Just because Carter's so handsome and full of fun and unconventional. He's always treated me with—"

"What the hell do you mean, always?" Jason jumped to his feet, sending the heavy leather chair screeching back on the parquet floor, the pen flying across the desk. "Have you been going out with him behind my back?"

"No," Lauren said with a gasp, the intensity of his reaction taking her totally by surprise. She staggered back several steps as Jason came tearing around the desk. "Evan brought him over a few times...when you were away on business this summer," she explained. "And we went to a couple of barbecues and beach parties at Carter's place. That's all."

He studied her intently for a moment as if carefully weighing the evidence of her guilt. From the half smile he gave her, she felt she'd been granted a suspended sentence. "I don't want you to see him anymore, Lauren. You'll only get into trouble," he said in stern but patient tones. "You're too young and inexperienced to be able to handle someone like Carter."

"Jason, I'm twenty years old," Lauren protested. "I have a right to decide who I want to see."

A crooked smile twisted his mouth. "No, you don't have the right. Not until you're twenty-one and I'm no longer your legal guardian. Until then, what happens to you is my responsibility, so I'll decide who's right for you and who's not."

He turned dismissively and walked over to his chair. "Since you're not going to the party, I suggest you change into something more...suitable." With one tug of his hand, he pulled the heavy leather chair back into place. "Dinner's at—"

"No!" Lauren interrupted for a change. "You're not going to stop me this time!" She was shaking from a barrage of emotions—disappointment, anger, fear—but she was determined to stand up to him once and for all. The startled look on his face gave her courage and a sense of deep satisfaction. "If I have to *walk* all the way to Carter's, I'm going to the party."

Lauren spun on her heel and made quickly for the door. With a few long-legged strides, Jason beat her to it. Slamming the door shut, he blocked it with his massive body. "Don't force me to do something drastic, Lauren," he warned grimly. It was the first time he'd ever threatened her. He stood there, towering over her, every muscle in his body taut, ready for action. She'd never realized how physically powerful he was, the potential for violence in him. She was never more aware of her own powerlessness. "I'm only trying to do what's right for you."

"What's right, that's all you care about!" Lauren cried, long-denied emotions exploding out of her control. "You can't stand to see me happy! You think I'm an unfeeling machine like you, but there's more to life than work and music! If it were up to you, I'd spend my whole life at the piano, all alone, without any friends, with no one to love me!"

"That's the last thing in the world I want for you," he objected. "The only reason I push you so hard sometimes is because I want you to have a life that's full, and—"

"No, you don't!" she yelled, shaking her head wildly. "You won't be satisfied until you've turned me into a famous, lonely, shriveled-up old maid with only a scrapbook full of—"

"Stop it!" Grabbing her by the shoulders, he shook her hard, as if to snap her out of the almost hysterical state she was in. But it was the unexpected warmth of his hands on her bare skin that shocked her back to herself.

They were both shaking visibly in the tense silence that hung, quivering, between them. They stared at each other as if they had never seen one another before.

With an abrupt, awkward motion, Jason released her. "Lauren, listen to me," he said urgently as she started to turn away from him. "Please." Unaccustomed to pleading, his voice cracked. She turned back to him.

Placing his hand lightly on her elbow, he led her over to the oxblood leather couch in front of the fireplace. Her legs were shaking so much, she was grateful for the chance to sit down. She felt emotionally drained.

"All I ever wanted was for you to be happy," Jason said, sinking down onto the couch next to her. "I've obviously gone about it the wrong way, but you've got to believe that." His voice was thick with regret, and a deep tenderness softened the lines of his rugged face, glowed in his dark eyes as they searched hers. Suddenly he was the Jason that Lauren once knew, and something turned over inside her.

"I don't want to see you get hurt, Lauren. That's why I don't want you to go out with Carter." When he spoke in that soft, deep tone, without his usual sarcasm, his voice was oddly musical, almost hypnotic. "I have no objection to your going to barbecues or beach parties, as long as it's with boys your own age."

"Carter's only eight years older than I am."

"But you're a very young twenty," he pointed out wryly, "and Carter's a very experienced twenty-eight."

"You're thirty-six and you go out with younger women," Lauren blurted out. She was surprised by the hint of indignation in her tone, the touch of jealousy.

A bemused smile flickered across his face. "How did you know that?"

"Gossip," she returned pointedly.

"Well, I don't go out with twenty-year-olds," he assured her. "And the women I go out with who *are* younger than I am are just as . . . experienced."

Lauren shifted uncomfortably in her seat. She'd never thought seriously about Jason and other women.

She'd taken it for granted that he would never marry. Now she wondered whether there was a woman in his life, and if he loved her.

"Besides, I have no illusions about them," he added with a trace of bitterness, "nor do they have any illusions about the nature of our—" he shrugged indifferently "—relationships, for want of a better term. Unlike your friend, Carter, I don't make promises I can't keep."

"But Carter—"

"Carter," he overrode her, "has no qualms whatsoever about taking advantage of a young girl who doesn't know the score. Or about dropping her flat afterward to go chasing after his next conquest."

"He's *not* like that," Lauren insisted, placing her hand on Jason's arm in an attempt to make him listen. "It's the girls who run after him, not the other way around. He can't help it if he's so attractive."

Jason pulled his arm away. "And is that what you want to be, Lauren?" he drawled sarcastically. "Another one of the girls who chase after Carter?" The rugged lines of his face had hardened again. There was no tenderness in his eyes now. "Is that how you want to end up, as another one of Carter's discarded playmates?"

"No!" She was hurt that he would think that of her. "Carter loves me. He's told me so."

He laughed, a short, sardonic laugh. "You and a few hundred others."

Lauren pulled herself up proudly. "He's asked me to marry him."

Jason went white under his tan, and every muscle in his powerful body stiffened. "Just how far has this thing with you and Carter gone?" he demanded. His tone was all the more chilling for being utterly devoid of feeling. "Have you gone to bed with him?"

"No, of course not," she murmured, looking away in embarrassment.

"But he's tried to get you into bed, hasn't he?" Reaching out abruptly, Jason grabbed Lauren's chin and jerked her face back to his. "Hasn't he?" he repeated angrily. For a moment, she was too stunned to react. If she didn't know him better, she would have thought that he was jealous.

"Tell me the truth!"

"Yes!" she admitted with pride. She was glad that *somebody* wanted her.

"That explains the marriage proposal," he said contemptuously. "Don't delude yourself. Carter doesn't love you. You're just a new experience for him." He released her with a twisted smile. "Once he's had you, it won't be long before he starts chasing after new conquests."

"That's not true," Lauren cried brokenly. "Carter loves me." Pushing herself up off the couch, she turned on him with all the hurt and anger that were in her. "Just because *you* can't love me doesn't mean that no one else can!"

"I don't love you?" he murmured incredulously. "Is that what you think?"

"All you've ever cared about is my talent, not me."

"Your talent *is* you," he insisted, getting to his feet in one powerful motion. "Your talent, your sensitivity, your—"

"Carter couldn't care less about my talent," Lauren declared as though that were something to be proud of. "He loves me as a woman."

Jason's eyes narrowed, and his hands clenched into fists. The potential for violence that Lauren had sensed in him before was almost palpable. "I doubt that Carter knows the meaning of the word love," he said harshly. "And when you grow up, Lauren, you'll realize that there are many ways to love. Sex is the least of them."

"Stop treating me like a child," she yelled. "I know what love is!"

"Do you?" He took a step toward her that was more like a stumble. "You mean . . . Carter?"

No, she didn't mean Carter. Carter wasn't the man she'd worshiped all these years. He wasn't the one person whose love and respect meant more to her than anything else in the world. "Yes, Carter!"

He went very still. His eyes were the scariest she'd ever seen them. "I don't believe you," he said finally, his voice as tight as a wire stretched to the breaking point. "You could never love someone like Carter."

"Well I do," she insisted defiantly. "And I am going to marry him."

"The hell you are," he bit out furiously. He took a threatening step toward her. "Not if I have anything to say about it."

"You don't. It's my life and my decision," she returned, refusing to back down even though she was shaking inside. "It has nothing to do with you."

"Nothing to do with me?" He laughed once. The bitter, lacerating sound cut right through her. "Have I cared about anything or anybody these last seven years besides you? Have I had any other life outside of you?" He moved in on her, his face contorted with an emotional intensity she would never have believed him capable of. "And you think I'm going to just stand by now and let you throw away yourself, your career, everything we've worked for, on a man like Carter?''

Her career, that was still all he cared about. "I don't care about my career anymore!" Tears burning behind her eyelids, Lauren turned and started to walk away, but Jason grabbed her arm, pulling her back roughly.

"You're not going to him," he vowed grimly. Before she could free herself, he reached out and grabbed her other arm, holding her captive. "I won't allow you to give yourself to a man who's incapable of appreciating the kind of woman you are. The woman *I've* made you!"

"Let go." Lauren fought to twist free of his grasp, but he was too strong for her. "Jason, you're hurting me."

"I don't understand you," he went on with a mixture of frustration and anger. "I've tried to give you everything you've ever wanted."

Except love, she thought ruefully.

"What else do you want?" He searched her eyes intensely. She lowered them before he could read the answer in their depths.

"Look at me!" Tightening his hold on her, he pulled her closer, so close she could feel the tension coiling every muscle in his body, the angry heat of his breath on her face. "What can Carter give you that I can't?" he asked, his voice raw.

It occurred to Lauren that Jason's question was that of a jealous lover, not of a legal guardian. She felt completely disoriented. "Carter makes me feel wanted and...and exciting to be with," she stammered. Her bare skin felt the heat emanating from Jason's body. The tangy scent of him, reminiscent of sandalwood—a scent she'd never noticed before—swirled around her senses. Her heart began pounding erratically. "I could be happy with Carter," she insisted a bit too desperately. "He makes everything fun and exciting."

"Excitement? Is that what you want?" Jason's fingers dug into Lauren's arms as he pulled her against him. "You don't have to run to Carter for excitement," he grated just before his mouth came down on hers.

Lauren was too overwhelmed to react. The burning crush of his mouth took her breath away; the powerful crush of his arms as they locked around her made it impossible to get her breath back. There was no tenderness in his kiss. He sought to dominate her totally, as if he meant to wipe out all other sensations but the bruising pressure of his mouth, the vibrant hardness of his body.

In an effort to recover, Lauren started to pull her head away. Jason's hand shot up her back to bury itself deep in her hair, holding her captive. His mouth moved roughly on hers, almost desperately, forcing her lips apart to admit the possessive thrust of his tongue. He moaned when he tasted her, the moan of a person whose hunger has been too great and endured for too long.

His arm slid down her back to press her into the feverish heat of him while his tongue moved inside her with deepening rhythmic thrusts, sending sensations she'd never known shivering through her.

Carter had never kissed her that way. His mouth had never burned, setting hers on fire. Raw emotion had never coiled the muscles of his arms, making her long to lose herself in his embrace. But the realization that it was Jason who was kissing her that way, Jason who was arousing such feelings in her, shocked and frightened Lauren.

She pressed frantic hands against his sides to push him away. His whole body contracted at her touch, sending an aftershock rippling through her. She could feel his thighs trembling against hers—even more than hers trembled. She stopped fighting him.

Her arms slipped around his back, and her mouth softened under his. He moaned with pleasure this time, and his tongue traced the inner softness of her mouth with long, slow, almost unbearably sensuous strokes. The moan she heard this time was her own. She melted against him.

How could this be happening, she wondered dazedly. When had desire become part of the love she'd always had for him? How long had it been buried inside her, waiting only to be released?

Her body surged passionately against his, eager for the feel and warmth of him. His kiss deepened, became consuming, shattering her with pleasure. Breathless, she clung to him, returning his kiss with all the love that was in her.

With a groan, Jason tore his mouth away from Lauren's. "Is this what you want?" he asked thickly, his ragged breath brushing her lips. "Is it exciting enough for you?"

"Yes," she breathed mindlessly. Her arms went up to twine around his neck. Now that she'd found him, she never wanted to lose him again.

"I realize this is the one area of your education that I've neglected," he murmured wryly. Bending his head, he bit the corner of her mouth, making her gasp. "But I see Carter has been giving you lessons."

"What?" Lauren's eyes fluttered open. She was about to tell him how painfully awkward and inexperienced she'd been with Carter, how he'd even teased her about it. The twisted smile she saw on Jason's face stopped her.

"Well, you don't have to go to Carter for lessons anymore," he promised darkly, his hands rushing up to claim her breasts. "If it's sex you want, I'll give it to you."

Lauren gasped soundlessly. She couldn't breathe from the pain twisting inside her. Jason lowered his mouth to hers again, but she shoved him back with more strength than she would have believed herself capable of. "You bastard!" Caught off balance, he staggered back against the edge of the leather couch and went sprawling across it. "You heartless, cold-blooded monster!"

Tears streaming down her face, Lauren ran out of the study, all the way down the hallway and through the back door leading onto the beach. She didn't stop running until she got to Carter's, and . . .

The stinging pain in her hands jolted Lauren abruptly back to the present. Unclenching her fists, she found that her nails had left livid, crescent-shaped marks in her palms. And she was always so careful with her hands!

She blinked several times as though she were just awakening from a deep sleep, then stared out the bay window. Twilight was beginning to tinge sky and water a silvery blue. Except for the pale, willowy beach grass swaying in the wind, the beach was deserted. Jason was probably jogging over to the lighthouse as he usually did.

God, but she dreaded seeing him again. She had to fight the impulse to grab her suitcases and bolt before he got back to the house. If it weren't for Aunt Clarissa, she would have bolted.

Lauren rubbed her hands together to ease their soreness. Only then did she realize that her palms were sweaty and her pulse was beating erratically. A rush of heat had shot through her when she remembered the way Jason had made love to her; it lingered still under her skin and in the core of her body.

"You'd better pull yourself together, girl," Lauren muttered impatiently under her breath as she hurried over to the piano. Sliding onto the bench, she flipped up the fall board. Music could affect her the way alcohol or tranquilizers affected other people: it took the rough edges off reality and helped her forget her problems.

Resting her fingers lightly on the keys, Lauren mentally skimmed through her repertoire. Nothing romantic or sentimental, thank you. She needed something bright and spirited to lift her out of her dark mood.

Dark moods brought Jason to mind again. Did he ever think about that night? she wondered. Would he find some way to throw it up to her? She certainly wouldn't put it past him. But even if he didn't, she was sure that what had happened that night would always be there between them.

Lauren lifted her hands high above the keyboard, then let them drop heavily, producing a chord of almost violent intensity as she tore into Chopin's Polonaise in A-flat. The heroic cry for freedom became hers. She was nearing the music's climax when her concentration was suddenly broken by the sound of a door being shoved open, sent slamming against a wall. She looked up from the keyboard to see an infuriated Jason come tearing into view.

"I told you I don't want anyone to touch her...piano," he finished lamely when he saw her. In less than a beat, he'd regained his control. "What the hell are you doing here?"

Four

It's nice to see you again, too, Jason," Lauren replied wryly. She slid her feet off the piano pedals; her legs were shaking even though she was still sitting.

"You weren't expected until Monday," said Jason, crossing the parlor with slow wary steps as if it were a mine field.

"I was able to cancel that magazine interview my manager had scheduled for tomorrow," Lauren explained. "I wanted to get here as soon as possible . . . to see Clarissa," she amended a bit too quickly.

"Why didn't you let me know?" He sounded annoyed at her for having taken him by surprise. Jason didn't like being taken by surprise. "I would have sent the car to pick you up at the airport."

"No need," she assured him. "I rented a car. Besides, I'm used to getting myself in and out of airports."

"So I see." Stopping under the arched entrance to the alcove, he reached out and flipped on the light switch.

Lauren blinked uncomfortably as the sudden burst of light from the brass and crystal chandelier hanging over the piano illuminated her. She preferred the shadowy reflection of twilight that had filled the room before; it made her feel safer, less exposed. And now, she could see Jason all too clearly.

He was still wearing the clothes he'd been jogging in: an olive-green sweater that clung damply to the sleek, hard muscles of his shoulders and chest, and a pair of khaki shorts. A fine sheen of perspiration made his bare legs, with their sprinkling of coarse dark hair, glisten. His face was flushed, his thick hair tangled from the wind, and several gleaming black strands spilled over the terry-cloth sweatband encircling his forehead. With his prominent cheekbones, slanted eyebrows and wide slash of a mouth, the headband gave him a raw, primitive look.

For a moment, Lauren was unable to reconcile the man who stood before her with the impeccably groomed, conservatively elegant man she remembered—or had she deliberately ignored this side of him before?

The still-fresh memory of those sleek, hard muscles wrapped around her, crushing her to him, the way his powerful thighs had trembled against hers, made heat surge under her skin again.

A slow smile curved Jason's mouth, and a perverse satisfaction gleamed hard in his eyes as they locked with hers. Lauren realized that he was also thinking about that night. She had the strangest feeling that he'd never stopped thinking about it. She tried to find something to say—anything—to break the unnerving silence between them. Her mouth was so dry, she would have been unable to utter it if she had.

A piercing howl suddenly shattered the silence, making Lauren jump: Killer had come prancing into the room in search of his master and had caught sight of Lauren. With another howl of delight, the dog tore across the room, past Jason, and threw himself on Lauren, almost knocking her off the bench.

"Down, Killer," Jason ordered, striding over to the piano while Lauren struggled to regain her balance under the Doberman's ecstatic assault.

"It's okay." Lauren laughed breathlessly as Killer, standing on his hind legs, placed a possessive paw on each of her shoulders, bringing his big fawn-and-black head to the same level as hers.

"I don't want him to dirty your clothes," said Jason, his eyes moving over her beige cashmere sweater and matching slacks. "He's just been running on the beach."

"It's only sand. It'll brush out." Lauren gave Killer a big hug. She was really delighted to see him again and even more grateful for the excuse to play with him rather than deal with Jason. She shrieked like a child as Killer began covering her face with long, slurpy kisses. "You're all wet!"

"He's probably been drinking," Jason explained apologetically. "You know how he sticks his whole face in the bowl." He suppressed a smile. "Killer, that's enough!"

Killer slanted his master a look to see how serious he was and just how much he'd let him get away with. He felt confident enough to sneak in another slurpy kiss that went from Lauren's chin clear up to her temple.

"Killer!" Lauren laughed again. "Was ever a dog so misnamed?" Jason watched as she wiped Killer's tawny muzzle with her long, expressive fingers. "You're just a pussycat." Caressing the top of his sleek black head, she dropped a kiss between the two tawny spots over his eyes. "Aren't you, huh?"

Killer growled a doggy yes and nuzzled Lauren's neck. Jason found himself wishing that he were a dog.

"Some terror you are," she teased, scratching the favorite spot behind his ears. "If a prowler broke in here, you'd probably kiss him to death." Agreeing with tiny gutteral sounds, Killer proceeded to wash Lauren's neck. "Look, he still does that," she said, pointing. When most dogs were happy to see someone, they wagged their tails; Killer wagged his whole backside.

Jason chuckled fondly. "Isn't he absurd?"

"Wouldn't it be nice if people had tails?" Lauren said, looking up at Jason suddenly.

The apprehension that had clouded her eyes when she looked at him before was gone; so was the tension straining her delicate features. Her lips were parted, soft and vulnerable, unknowingly sensuous. The light spilling over her shoulder-length platinum hair and long bangs created a halo effect around her exquisitely shaped face. But her translucent skin and enormous sea-green eyes glowed from an inner light.

Desire went through Jason like a shot of adrenaline, making his heartbeat quicken, ripping through the defenses he'd so carefully erected against her. He had to force himself to concentrate, to remember what she'd just asked him.

"If people had tails?" he managed sardonically. "What for?"

"So they wouldn't be able to hide their feelings," she replied as if the logic were obvious. "You can always tell when a dog is happy to see you by the way he wags his tail."

"No, it would never work with people," Jason said without hesitation. "They'd just get specially designed clothes made to cover their tails."

"Why?"

"Because people can't afford to show their feelings." He couldn't believe that they were having this conversation. But he was willing to discuss the relative merits of wombat tails if that would keep the fearful look out of her eyes.

"You're probably right," Lauren agreed with a rueful smile. Killer's growl of complaint prompted her to resume scratching behind his ear. Pressing the side of his head against her hand, Killer closed his eyes in sheer ecstasy.

"That's enough, dog," Jason muttered playfully. "You're downright obscene." Reaching over, he patted Killer on the head, brushing Lauren's hand unintentionally. She pulled her hand away as if he'd skinned her. The light went out of her eyes.

Jason felt something wrench inside him. Turning abruptly, he walked away. "Over here, Killer," he ordered, his voice hard. "Now!"

The Doberman's ears twitched, then flattened against his head. Springing off Lauren, he hurried over to his master, his tail between his legs.

"Atta boy," Jason murmured with a roughly apologetic pat on the shoulder.

His black velvet ears standing up proudly again, Killer sank gracefully to the floor at Jason's feet. Crossing one long, elegant paw over the other, he waited to see what was going to happen next.

"Have you seen Clarissa yet?" asked Jason, his voice neutral.

"No," Lauren replied, trying to match his tone. She felt a perfect fool for having overreacted and hoped Jason had been too involved with Killer to notice the effect his slightest touch had on her. "The nurse said she was sleeping."

"You can see her at dinner," he tossed over his shoulder as he turned to leave the room. "Dinner's still at seven, if you care to join us."

"What's wrong with Clarissa?" Lauren asked, genuinely concerned. "It's not anything . . . serious, is it?"

"I wish I knew." Jason turned back with an uncharacteristically defeated sigh. "She went into the hospital a month ago for what the doctors claimed was a minor operation. They keep assuring me that she's all right now, but she hasn't been out of bed since."

"Why didn't you call me when she first went to the hospital?" Lauren demanded. "I would have come back immediately."

A sarcastic smile twisted his hard mouth. "I didn't think you cared."

"That's not fair, Jason! You know how much I've always loved Clarissa. She's the—"

"I also know that you chose to make your own life away from us, from her," he cut her off coldly. "The only reason I called you at all was because Clarissa begged me to. I was against it. I still am."

It was the first time he'd spoken to her in his legal-guardian tone of voice. But Lauren was no longer his ward or his pupil. She sent him a cool smile. "I see. I've made my bed; now I have to lie in it. Is that it?"

"That's right," he shot back. "And with the partner of your choice."

Lauren tensed and looked away.

Sensing that he'd hit a nerve, Jason moved in on her. "How is our handsome, fun-loving, unconventional Carter by the way? I see you haven't brought him with you."

"No," Lauren confirmed, her voice barely audible.

"How very wifely and trusting of you," he drawled, stopping directly beside her. "Or was he busy elsewhere?"

Lauren forced herself to meet Jason's eyes. "Carter and I are divorced. I thought you knew that."

"No, I didn't," he murmured, clearly thrown. "I'm ... sorry."

A brittle laugh escaped her. "No, you're not. I'm sure you couldn't be more delighted." She shrugged indifferently. "You were right. He was everything you said he was."

Jason realized instantly that Lauren's indifference was an act; he could see the pain reflected deep in her eyes. That was what he'd hoped for these last four years—it was all he could hope for—that she was hurting as much as he was. Yet seeing her unhappiness now tore at something inside him.

"And he did everything to me you said he would," she finished unsteadily. "That should give you some satisfaction."

"No, it doesn't," Jason admitted, to his own surprise. "I'm not sorry about the divorce. You should never have married him in the first place. But I am very sorry that you've been hurt."

Lauren's soft lips parted in amazement. How could a man be so cold and unforgiving one moment and so warm and understanding the next? Would she ever be able to figure him out?

"I warned you," he went on with a mixture of anger and regret. "Why wouldn't you listen to me? Why did you have to run away?" He sank down beside her on the piano bench. "I was only trying to protect you," he murmured, his warm breath brushing her startled face. "I knew that you would end up getting hurt. That's why I—"

His voice broke off, and his eyes locked with hers. Lauren could see everything that had happened between them that night burning in their dark depths. Though she tried, she was unable to break their hold or stop the memories that flooded her mind and senses, threatening to overwhelm her.

She took a long, steadying breath and inhaled the salty fragrance of sea air mingling with the male sweat that clung, gleaming, to his skin. The breath caught in her throat. A sudden, intense longing for him welled up inside her as it had that night, frightening her.

"That's why I—" Jason started to explain somewhat guiltily again.

Jumping to her feet, Lauren cut him off angrily. "Why you had to make me feel cheap and dirty? If it hadn't been for you, I would never have married Carter!"

"What?"

With a silent curse at herself for having blurted out the truth, Lauren moved quickly from behind the bench.

With one lithe motion, Jason was on his feet. "What the hell do you mean by that?"

Turning her back on him, Lauren walked over to Killer, whose sleek head had shot up at the first sound of angry voices. She gave him a reassuring pat.

"I didn't come here to relive the past, Jason," she informed him coolly. "I know you don't want me here. The only reason I am here is because Clarissa needs me." Standing halfway across the room from him made it easier for Lauren to appear calmer than she was. "Since we'll be living in the same house for a while, I think we should try to get along, for her sake. I'll do my best to stay out of your way, and I'd appreciate it if you'd do the same."

Jason continued to stare at Lauren, trying to decipher what was going on in her mind. Finally, he asked, "How long are you planning on staying?"

"As long as Clarissa needs me," she replied, annoyed that he would have to ask, but grateful that he'd decided not to pursue their previous conversation. "I have only two more concerts booked this season: one at the end of the month in Philadelphia, and the other at the beginning of next month in Boston."

"I didn't realize you'd be staying that long," he said, his voice oddly subdued. "I'm sure Clarissa will be very pleased."

"I'm glad somebody will be," she couldn't resist tossing back at him. The strangest look flared in his eyes, tightened the deeply etched lines around his mouth. If she didn't know him better, she would have thought her comment had hurt him. "I'd arranged months ago to take some time off," she rattled on. "I'm overdue for a vacation, and I was planning on using that time to finish working on a new piece for my repertoire."

"I had the piano tuned for you." His voice and face were expressionless once more. "I knew you'd need to practice every day."

"Yes, I heard." It was just like him to take care of everything for her. She smiled gratefully. "Thanks."

"De nada," he drawled sarcastically.

The smile died on Lauren's lips; so did the good feeling she'd momentarily felt toward him. She was sorry now that she'd tried to be nice to him, and she promised herself not to try again. She turned and quickly made for the archway that separated the music room from the parlor. "It's getting late. I'd like to shower and change before seeing Clarissa."

"What new piece are you working on?" asked Jason, his tone conversational as he followed her, Killer at his heels.

Lauren hesitated for just a fraction of a second. "Beethoven. The *Emperor* Concerto."

"The *Emperor*?" He didn't bother to hide his amazement.

"I think I'm ready to tackle it," she insisted as though she expected him to give her an argument about it. She continued walking quickly ahead of him through the parlor. "I've been working on it for over a year. Another month or two should do it."

"I don't doubt it," he agreed.

Lauren slanted Jason a defensive look over her shoulder and was surprised to find that he wasn't being sarcastic for a change. "Not after hearing you play the Polonaise before with such power," he added sincerely. "No wonder I didn't recognize your touch."

"My touch *has* changed," Lauren allowed dryly. Lyrical and romantic pieces had always come easily to her, but more dramatic works that demanded assertiveness, even aggression, had always been a problem—but not anymore. "That's because *I've* changed." Stopping next to her suitcases, she slid him a confident smile.

He ignored her smile; instead he searched her face intently. "You've been through a lot in the past four years," he said, his voice grim. "Haven't you?"

He could still read her through and through, Lauren realized, and it unnerved her. She managed a carefree shrug. "I guess it's all part of growing up." Turning away from his too perceptive gaze, Lauren walked over to the door.

She took a long, steadying breath, and when she turned to face him again, she appeared sure of herself. "There's something you should realize right now, Jason. I'm not the same person who left here four years ago." She pulled the door open and held it for him. "And I won't be treated the same way. I'm used to making my own decisions now and running my own life."

"I've noticed that," he returned dryly.

"You're going to have to accept it as well."

An ironic smile flickered across his face. "I have no problem with that. The only problem I've ever had with you was trying to get you to stand up for yourself." He started toward her. "That's why I had to push so hard sometimes, to keep you from withdrawing into that shell of yours, to force you to fight back."

Lauren's large eyes opened even wider. She'd always assumed that he was merely expressing his disapproval of her. She'd never seen his deliberate goading in that light before, and it left her speechless.

"One thing's for sure," Jason went on as he waved Killer out the door before him. "You've turned into one hell of a woman. You could have been just beautiful but frivolous and empty-headed. Instead, you're also talented and independent. That's more than any man could hope for in one woman." A sardonic smile slashed his mouth. "I must have done something right."

With that, Jason turned and walked proudly out the door, leaving Lauren totally stunned.

Five

The door to Aunt Clarissa's bedroom was wide open, as was the door to the guest room directly across the hall, where the 24-hour nurse Jason had hired was staying. Lauren could see the woman sitting, as stiff as her starched white uniform, in front of the blaring television set. A barrage of gunshots rang out just as Lauren was knocking on Clarissa's door, followed by the sound of screeching tires as a car crashed and burst into flames.

Lauren shook her head with an impatient sigh. She assumed both doors were open so that Clarissa could call the nurse if she needed her, but she didn't see how the woman could hear her call with all that racket. Lauren knocked on her aunt's door again, loudly, in order to be heard over the brain-piercing scream of police sirens.

Sitting propped up against a mound of pillows, Aunt Clarissa looked up from the historical novel she was reading. She gasped aloud and the book slid out of her hands onto the covers. "Laurie, what a wonderful surprise!"

"I tried to get here as soon as I could." Closing the door behind her, Lauren rushed over to her aunt. "It's so good to see you again." Sitting down next to her on the bed, she gave Clarissa a big hug and was shocked to feel the bones of her rib cage through her flannel nightgown.

"Oh, Laurie, I've missed you so much," Clarissa said shakily when she fell back against the pillows, her eyes brimming with tears.

Clarissa's face was also thinner than Lauren remembered, and terribly drawn. Her faded blond hair was pulled back severely into a single braid hanging down her back, adding to her gaunt look. Her usually porcelain skin was sickbed-yellow, and her blue eyes looked washed out, as though she'd cried all the color out of them.

Lauren forced a smile to hide her concern. "I've missed you, too," she managed to say over the lump in her throat. Impulsively she grabbed her aunt's hands and squeezed them warmly. They felt like twigs under her supple fingers. She released them carefully, and they fluttered down to the covers as if they lacked the energy needed to sustain them. "How are you, Clarissa?"

"I'm fine now that you're here." She smiled the radiant smile of hers that Lauren had always loved, and it lit up her wan face. "It's so good to have you home again."

"Home," Lauren repeated softly, and the word stuck with the lump in her throat. Yes, this was still the only home she'd ever known, she realized ruefully. Blinking back the tears, she turned to look around the room she'd spent so many happy hours in.

Clarissa's bedroom, a mixture of antique prints and patterns in the crispest blue and white, had always reminded Lauren of an English country cottage. The white four-poster bed was trimmed in blue, and tiny bluebells ran riot over the white bedspread that matched the overstuffed armchair next to the bed. Cobalt-blue tiles faced the cozy fireplace in one corner, and the blue-and-white checkered fabric that spilled over the vanity, its long white fringe brushing the floor, echoed the drapes flanking the white shutters on the windows. Victorian prints hung on the fabric-covered walls, and several needlepoint rugs, blending the flowers of a country garden, lay scattered about the parquet floor.

"It's great to be home," Lauren admitted, turning back to her aunt.

"Jason told me that you'd come sooner than we'd expected," Clarissa said, her eyes filled with gratitude. "But why didn't you have dinner with us? Jason's been having dinner here in my room—whenever he doesn't stay over in Boston—to make sure that I eat."

"Well, I had a big lunch, so I wasn't hungry, and I wanted to unpack and get settled in." She hated to admit that she'd really been too shaken up at seeing Jason to be able to face him again so soon. "Besides, I wanted to be alone with you so we could talk girl talk, the way we used to."

"But you did see Jason?" her aunt asked anxiously. "You talked to him?"

"Yes."

"And everything's all right between you now?"

"I think so," Lauren replied after a moment's hesitation.

The anxious look remained fixed on Clarissa's face as she studied her niece intently. "You don't know how much Jason missed you, Laurie."

"Jason missed me? The only reason he called me was because you begged him to," she blurted out with more bitterness than she'd intended. "That's what he told me."

"Of course, that's what he would say." Clarissa managed a wan smile. "You didn't expect him to tell you how much he loves and misses you, did you? I thought you knew Jason better than that." She sank back against the mound of pillows with a weary sigh. "He's been impossible to live with these past four years."

Lauren had to laugh in spite of herself. "I can believe that, all right."

"I really mean it, Laurie. It broke my heart to see how unhappy he was," Clarissa insisted, making Lauren look away uncomfortably. "I don't think you know how much you hurt him when you ran away with—"

"I see you're working on a new doll," Lauren interrupted. Jumping up from the bed, she stepped over to the large wicker sewing basket resting on the overstuffed armchair.

"No, not really," Clarissa said with a regretful sigh. "I've been meaning to finish it, but I don't seem to have the energy."

The half-finished cloth doll, arms and legs sprawling over the edge of the basket where it had been tossed, had a decidedly abandoned look to it. Only the first layer of synthetic hair had been attached to its head, making it look as though it were going bald. With only one shiny black button for an eye, its face appeared somewhat lopsided. But the rest of its features had been completed, so that a trace of personality was already evident.

Each of Clarissa's dolls had a distinct personality of its own, Lauren remembered, and making them had always given her aunt great pleasure and satisfaction. "I'm sure it's going to be adorable, Clarissa. You should finish it."

"Yes, I should," she murmured guiltily. "I just can't seem to do anything these days. I don't know why, but I'm exhausted all the time."

"Then you should wait until you're well again."

"But the doctor says I *am* well," she returned with a frustrated sigh. "I really don't know what's the matter with me."

"Knowing you, I'm sure you were working too hard. That's probably why you got sick in the first place."

"No, not really. With you gone, and then Evan..." Tears welled up in her eyes, and she was unable to continue.

Lauren moved quickly back to the bed. "Clarissa, what's the matter?"

"Oh, I don't know what's wrong with me." Reaching over, she pulled a couple of tissues out of the box on the night table. "I cry at the drop of a hat these days."

"Is it Evan?" Lauren asked, concerned. "Is he in trouble again?"

Clarissa shook her head as she blew her nose with tiny, ladylike sounds. "Evan and Jason had a terrible fight. It was really Evan's fault, in a way," she admitted grudgingly as she dabbed at her eyes. "But I haven't seen or heard from him in over a year and... and I've been no help at all to Jason lately. I just hate being a burden to him."

"You could never be a burden to Jason," Lauren assured her. "He cares about you too much."

"Yes, I know, but it's just not fair to him. I'm sure he's only staying on here because of me . . . because he feels sorry for me." She looked up at Lauren with wet, imploring eyes. "But I am going to get up soon, you'll see."

"Of course you will."

With a heavy sigh, Clarissa dabbed at her eyes with a tissue. "I say that every day. Tomorrow I'm going to get up. But then I'm always so tired."

"What do you think it is?" Lauren asked, tugging the armchair close to the bed.

"I can't sleep nights. Night after night, I just lie here. I can't turn my mind off." She laughed brokenly. "You know what a silly mind I have."

"You do not. And you've got to stop putting yourself down, Clarissa." Placing the sewing basket on the floor, Lauren sank down into the armchair. "What do you think about when you can't sleep?"

"Oh, nothing...everything...the past mostly." Her head fell back heavily against the pillows as if pulled down by its own weight. "I keep going over and over all the mistakes I've made, all the wasted years."

"My God, Clarissa, that's the worst thing you could do." Lauren leaned over the edge of the bed in her attempt to get through to her aunt. "There's no point in reliving a past you can't change. It's the surest way to make yourself sick."

"I keep hoping I'll find out why things turned out this way." Her pale eyes filled with helpless tears again. "I've always tried so hard to make this a happy home, but everyone keeps leaving and never coming back. First Laura, then you, now Evan.''

Guilt and regret twisted inside Lauren when she realized how she'd unintentionally hurt her aunt who had always been so good to her. ''But we've all got to make our own life, Clarissa,'' she murmured apologetically.

''Oh, I know. I didn't mean it that way,'' she returned, reaching for another tissue. ''But I'd thought we'd always be a family in spite of all our differences. That we'd still get together, like other families, for the holidays and summer vacations and...'' Shaking her head hopelessly, she wiped away fresh tears. ''Oh, I'm sorry to burden you with all this, Laurie, on your first day home.''

''Don't be. You know you can always talk to me.'' Reaching over impulsively, Lauren put her hand on her aunt's frail arm. ''Things are going to be different now, Clarissa, I promise.'' She gave her a reassuring smile. ''I'm home now, and I'm going to see to it that Evan comes home, too.''

''Oh, could you do that?'' Clarissa asked breathlessly. Just the thought of seeing Evan again made her face light up. ''It would mean so much to me.''

''Yes, I will,'' she promised, squeezing Clarissa's arm softly before releasing it. ''I'll talk to Jason about it first thing tomorrow.''

''Would you? You're still the only one Jason listens to.''

Lauren laughed harshly. ''Are you serious?''

''Jason would do anything for you, Lauren, you know that,'' Clarissa insisted. ''You should have heard him go on and on about you at dinner. He's so proud of you.''

''That wasn't the impression I got.''

"Well, you know how Jason hides his emotions, but that doesn't mean he doesn't feel things deeply. I sometimes think it's *because* he feels things so deeply." Sitting up, Clarissa leaned toward Lauren. "He may not always show it, but Jason cares for you very much, Laurie. I've never known Jason to care for anyone as he does for you."

Her aunt's obviously sincere words bothered Lauren in a way she couldn't understand. A part of her still wanted to believe that Jason loved her, she realized resentfully, even though she knew he didn't, that he never had.

"Clarissa, Jason doesn't care about me," she returned defensively. "The only reason he took such an interest in me is because he wanted to make me the concert pianist he'd always dreamed of being."

"Oh, you're wrong, Laurie," she said, shaking her head forcefully. "If you only knew how much you hurt him when you ran off and eloped with Carter. I've never seen Jason so...devastated."

The thought of Jason being devastated over her left Lauren speechless.

With a heavy sigh, Clarissa sank back against the pillows and closed her eyes as if all their talking had exhausted her.

Lauren sprang up from the chair with concern, her mixed emotions about Jason forgotten. "Clarissa, are you all right?"

With a wan smile, she opened her eyes. "Now that you're back home, everything's going to be all right, isn't it?" Lauren's nod made her smile widen. "And you will make it up with Jason?"

"I will. And I'll see to it that Evan makes it up with him, too. I promise."

"Oh, that would make me so happy." Tears misted her eyes again, but they were tears of joy this time. "Then we can all be a family again."

"Yes," Lauren promised, swallowing the lump in her throat. "But you've got to get better, Clarissa. You don't want Evan to see you this way."

"Oh, no!"

"Then I think you should rest now." Quickly, Lauren smoothed out the covers and tucked her aunt in. "Is there anything I can get you before I go?"

"No." She smiled gratefully. "I think I'll be able to sleep now."

"Good." Bending over, Lauren kissed Clarissa softly on the cheek. "Call me if you need anything, okay?" Making a mental note to tell the nurse to lower the volume of the television set—something she knew Clarissa was too retiring to do, something she herself would have been unable to do a few years ago—Lauren started for the door.

"Laurie?" Clarissa called out anxiously. "You won't tell Jason what I told you . . . about his being so devastated when you ran away?"

Stopping in front of the door, Lauren looked back at her aunt with a wry smile. "No, of course not."

"And Laurie?" she added insistently as Lauren was about to step through the open door. "I know how impossible Jason can be at times, but please be patient with him. He loves you very much."

"I'll...I'll try," Lauren stammered. When she closed the door behind her, her hand was shaking.

Aunt Clarissa's words kept playing over and over in Lauren's mind like the haunting echo of a piece of music whose secrets she was having trouble unraveling.

The few times she saw Jason in the next four days, Lauren studied him intently. But she could find nothing in his manner to indicate that he'd missed her so terribly or that he was glad she was home again, let alone that he loved her. If anything, he seemed even more uncomfortable in her presence than she was in his. And though they both went out of their way to be polite to one another, there was always an undercurrent of tension between them—of unspoken words and hidden emotions—that left her feeling confused and uncertain.

Lauren was sure that the two nights Jason had stayed over in the town house he'd always kept in Boston were as much to avoid her as to take care of business.

Knowing how difficult it was for Clarissa to deal with any kind of unpleasantness, how desperately she'd always tried to keep the peace in the family, Lauren finally decided that Jason's love for her had been sheer wishful thinking on her aunt's part.

She told herself that she no longer cared whether Jason loved her or not anyway because she no longer needed or wanted his love. But she had told herself that so many times, only to be upset by the mere thought of him, that she could no longer trust herself.

Lauren shook her head impatiently, annoyed at herself for not having more control over her thoughts and feelings. She continued staring, unseeing, out her bedroom window. She hadn't felt this confused and unsure of herself in four years. Taking another sip of her morning coffee, she forced herself to concentrate on the view to see if she could at least figure out what the weather was going to be like that day.

There wasn't much hope there, either, she realized as she studied the uncertain gray sky, the silvery light and moody shadows the Cape was famous for. From her bedroom, situated at the front of the house, Lauren could see the moors in the distance. She was reminded that Truro had been named after the region in Cornwall, England, because of its rugged plains and wild moors that rose and fell from Cape Cod Bay to the Atlantic.

A persistent fog frosting still covered the moors, and patches of snow were visible among the untamed shrubbery and wild brambles that were still a dull wintry brown. The gusting wind that shaped and bent them could be heard moaning under the eaves of the old Victorian house, rattling windowpanes and banging a loose shutter.

The pervasive desolate feeling of life being held in suspension, of a long, hard winter clinging relentlessly, enveloped Lauren. Still in her nightgown, she shivered and gulped down some more hot coffee. She wondered whether spring would ever come again.

Lauren was so caught up in her thoughts, she was unaware that Jason had just stopped in front of the half-open sliding doors that separated the bedroom from the parlor.

Held by the sight of Lauren in her nightgown, Jason stood there as if nailed to the floor. Poised in midair, his hand refused to knock on the door, as he'd intended, to let her know he was there. He knew the longer he looked at her, the harder it would be for him to deal with her, and it would be all the more wrenching to leave for Boston afterward. He bitterly regretted her being there. But he couldn't stop looking at her any more than he could stop himself from wanting her.

The silvery light spilling through the window heightened the glow of Lauren's skin, the delicacy of her features, and made her platinum hair shimmer. She was wearing an ivory satin nightgown that was cut as simply as a slip, without lace or fancy embroidery. The very simplicity of the cut made it impossible to hide any flaws in her body. There were no flaws.

Her breasts were high and firm, beautifully shaped. He remembered how perfectly they had fit in his hands. Tension began coiling inside him, and Jason warned himself that he would drive himself crazy if he kept that up. But his gaze moved hungrily down her slender waist, over the exquisitely feminine curve of her hips, as he recalled how she'd felt in his arms, the way her body had melted against his.

The coil tightened, sending heat pulsing through him. He realized that no matter what he did, he would never get her out of his blood. It was only with the greatest effort of will that he was able to stop himself from becoming fully aroused. He'd certainly had enough practice.

Jason wondered what Lauren could be thinking of so intensely. There was a certain sadness in the way she stood there clutching her coffee cup, a sense that she felt herself to be utterly alone, and it reminded him of the first time he'd seen her.

Looking now at her slender arms, delicate shoulders and long, coltish legs, he could still see traces of the young girl he'd known. And there was an innocence about her that went beyond her innate shyness, as though she were still trembling on the brink of womanhood, had not yet been awakened to its dark mysteries and pleasures.

Since she'd been married to a man like Carter, Jason reminded himself bitterly, that was hardly possible. He knocked on the door, much louder than he'd intended, making Lauren jump. She turned her startled face toward him, and he saw that fearful look come into her eyes.

Would she ever forgive him for what he'd done, he wondered miserably. Wasn't it enough that he couldn't forgive himself?

"I didn't mean to startle you," Jason managed to say coolly. "You told Annie, the new housekeeper, that you wanted to see me about something?"

"Yes, I did," Lauren said, then stood there dumbly. All she could think of was that she was half-dressed in front of him; she felt naked. She set her coffee cup down on the windowsill and hurried to the foot of the bed to get her matching peignoir. "I'll finish dressing, and we can talk about it over breakfast."

"I've already had breakfast," he informed her dryly. "I'm on my way to the office and I'm running late."

"This will only take a moment." Quickly retrieving her peignoir, Lauren turned her back on Jason. Even though he was standing clear across the room, she was intensely aware of him. Her hand was trembling as she slid it into one of the long, flowing sleeves.

An amused smile tugged at the corners of Jason's mouth as he watched Lauren. She was obviously unaware that she was just as exciting to look at from the back. And the way she was acting, you would have thought that no man had ever seen her in a nightgown before. Yet something kept him respectfully by the door, waiting until she was ready.

She'd buttoned the peignoir all the way up to the top. It covered her nightgown, but the soft satiny fabric clung to every curve of her body and swayed sensuously around her long legs as she turned. Jason muttered a silent curse.

"I'm flying back to Boston," he told her, making sure that his tone of voice wouldn't give him away.

"But you just got back," she said, taking several steps toward him, satin rustling around her ankles.

"I've let a lot of things slide at the office because of Clarissa," he explained smoothly, "and now that you're here I'm trying to catch up, so..." He paused because she'd just shot him the strangest look. He had the feeling that she didn't believe him.

Well, *she* was the one who'd told him to stay out of her way, Jason reminded himself resentfully, even though he knew he was really doing it to make it easier on himself. "So I'll be staying over in Boston again tonight and on Thursday," he went on matter-of-factly. "I'll be back Friday afternoon."

Jason thought he caught a flash of disappointment in Lauren's eyes. He told himself that he was just seeing things.

"I don't want to make you miss your plane," she said, looking away, "but it is important. It's about Clarissa."

"Don't worry about it. I'll catch a later plane." His shrug was one of unconcern. "If it's about Clarissa, I'll make the time."

Her aunt was right about one thing, Lauren was forced to admit: Jason was a deeply caring man. He was always there when you needed him. But then, no one knew that better than she. She sent him a grateful smile. "Thanks, Jason."

"De nada," he returned sarcastically.

Normally, Lauren would have reacted defensively to Jason's sarcasm, but after her talk with Clarissa, it merely saddened her that he felt he had to hide the sensitive side of his nature. Her smile widened, became warm and inviting. "Well, come on in then."

Jason was still standing by the door, looking very businesslike in his dark blue pin-striped suit and very uncomfortable. It suddenly occurred to her that he might be uncomfortable in her presence for the same reason she was in his. She forgot to breathe.

Jason took a single wary step into Lauren's bedroom, looking around as though he'd never seen it before. The old-fashioned Victorian look of the room, all soft pastels and delicate lace and ruffles, was as exquisitely feminine as Lauren. And made Jason feel even bigger and clumsier than usual.

"Do you have everything you need?" he asked stiffly. "Are you comfortable here?"

"Yes, very," Lauren replied sincerely. "I've always loved this room, and I find I'm still mad for Laura Ashley." With a wave of her hand, she indicated the delicate floral fabric that covered the walls and made up the flowing drapes framing the transparent lace panels on the windows.

Tiny bouquets of sugar-pink roses caught up with pale-green ribbons spilled over the ivory background, reminiscent of early spring in a country garden. The wall-to-wall carpet was also ivory and reflected the gray winter light streaming through the ceiling-high windows, suffusing the room with a soft, hazy glow. The white iron bed was all graceful curves and intricate flowering designs, and folded at the foot was an antique-lace bedspread that fell in a profusion of ruffles to the floor.

Jason could see the indentation of Lauren's body in the white linen sheets where the covers had been tossed aside. An image of her lovely body sprawled across the bed, her platinum hair spilling over the lace-edged pillows, flashed in his mind, sending a jolt of desire through him. Tearing his gaze away, he made a thorough study of the Victorian lithographs hanging over the fireplace.

Lauren laughed suddenly. "You let me redecorate this room as a birthday present when I was eighteen, remember?"

What Jason remembered was how excited Lauren had been with the project, how happy she'd looked when she first showed him the finished room. Some of that happiness glowed in her sea-green eyes now as she looked over at him.

"Yes," he said tightly. "I remember." But he didn't want to remember. It was painful enough when he did it on his own. "What did you want to tell me about Clarissa?" he asked, bringing them back to the present, bleak as it was.

"Oh, yes," she murmured, as though she'd forgotten her original intention; when she spoke again, her voice and manner were impersonal. "Jason, I think Clarissa's illness is more psychological than physical at this point." She paused and smiled self-consciously. "I know this may sound silly to you, but I think she's literally sick with loneliness."

"It doesn't sound silly at all."

Lauren's eyes widened in surprise. He sounded as if he were speaking from personal experience. She'd always believed that Jason needed no one.

"So?" he asked brusquely as he started toward her, clearly annoyed at having given himself away.

"Well, she misses Evan terribly," Lauren explained. "You know how much he's always meant to her." In her attempt to get through to him, she took several steps toward him, the satiny fabric sliding over her body as she moved.

Jason halted by an embroidered Victorian footstool; Lauren continued over to him. "Won't you make it up with him, for Clarissa's sake, and let him come home again?"

"I've never stopped Evan from coming home anytime he wants to," Jason protested. "Where did you get that idea?"

"Clarissa implied that—"

"I know I'm always cast as the villain in the piece," he cut her off sardonically, "but that was Evan's choice, not mine."

"Do you have any idea where I can reach him?"

"I know he's living somewhere in New York," said Jason, trying to look at Lauren without seeing how achingly lovely she was. He was unable to manage it. "I'll have my secretary track down his address and phone number and call you this afternoon."

"I'd really appreciate it." There was warmth in Lauren's eyes as she looked up at him, and her lips were parted, soft and unbearably sensuous. "I know it'll make a big difference to Clarissa."

Jason smiled that twisted smile of his, making Lauren wonder what she'd said wrong this time. "I'm sure it'll make *all* the difference," he drawled. "God knows, *I* haven't been able to help."

The bitterness in Jason's tone took Lauren completely by surprise and hurt her somehow. Impulsively she reached out and grabbed his arm just as he was turning to walk away. "That's not true, Jason. I don't know what Clarissa would have done without you." She squeezed his arm warmly and felt powerful muscles tauten under her hand, reminding her of how every muscle in his body had been taut with emotion that time he'd made love to her.

Jason pulled his arm away. "I'm sure Dr. Evan will complete the cure," he said with a sarcastic smile. He checked his watch, as if that were the reason he'd pulled his arm away so abruptly. The last thing he wanted was her pity. "Is that it?" he asked evenly. "I'd like to catch the next plane out."

Still recovering from the feel of him, the rush of memories sweeping over her, Lauren's hand remained poised in midair. "Yes," she murmured, "that's it." Her hand moved to tuck a stray lock of hair behind one ear.

Unbelievably fragrant hair, Jason recalled. "If you need anything, you know where to contact me," he got out, and he started for the door before he did something he was sure he would regret. "I know we need to talk some more...about Clarissa. I'm sorry I can't give you any more time today."

"I understand," Lauren replied, her voice barely audible, her tone indefinably sad.

Jason stopped in the doorway and slanted Lauren a long look over his shoulder. "I'll be back on Friday. Let me take you out to dinner, and we can talk all you like."

He was out the door before Lauren even knew how to answer.

Six

The restaurant Jason selected for their dinner was one of the best in P'town, as Cape Codders always referred to Provincetown. It was famous for its patio dining and rooftop dancing, and though still enclosed in its winter shell of protective glass, it afforded an extensive view of the picturesque harbor.

The driftwood-paneled dining room was hung with antique ships' helms, harpoons and other whaler's tools. Authentic Portuguese fishnets were strung along the ceiling among puffed-up blowfish that, to Lauren, looked somewhat astonished at having been turned into lighting fixtures.

Since the restaurant refused reservations on weekends, there was a long line of people waiting when Jason and Lauren came in, and the bar was three-deep in patrons whose names had been entered on the waiting list. Lauren had already resigned herself to eating dinner at ten o'clock, when the headwaiter, spotting Jason as he checked their coats, left a couple in midcomplaint to come rushing over to him.

"Mr. Caldwell, it's good to see you again." His tone managed to be servile and snobbish at the same time. "Bernard told me that you'd called."

"Thanks for accepting my reservation, Malcolm."

"For you, anytime, Mr. Caldwell." From his tall, gangly height, the headwaiter looked down his long nose at Lauren. He scrutinized her pale-blue silk dress, noting how it softly outlined the feminine curves of her breasts and hips before falling in a swirl around her knees. She had the feeling he was comparing her to the other women Jason had brought there. She suddenly felt as if they were on a date!

The haughty headwaiter finished giving her the once-over; a thin-lipped smile indicated his reluctant approval. "Your table is ready." With a theatrical sweep of his hand, he motioned for them to follow him.

A murmur of discreet outrage preceded them down the long line of waiting patrons, but Lauren noticed several women glancing at Jason with open admiration. He did undeniably project a sense of power and authority. The dark-blue, three-piece suit he wore was obviously custom-made, the European cut understated but elegant. With his craggy features and tall, powerful body, he made most of the other men in the place look like boys.

Lauren concentrated on following the headwaiter past the hundred-gallon tank literally crawling with live lobsters and over to a corner table in front of the glass wall.

"This is perfect, Malcolm." Jason smiled approvingly and slipped the hovering headwaiter a twenty-dollar bill. "Thanks."

"Anytime, Mr. Caldwell," Malcolm purred. One hand slid the twenty unobtrusively into his side pocket, while the other sliced through the air with several staccato movements as he motioned a waiter over to their table; he might have been conducting the opening to Beethoven's Fifth. "Enjoy your dinner."

After seating Lauren in the mate's chair, Jason took the captain's chair directly across the table from her. There was an awkward pause after they'd both settled themselves, and then Jason's eyes scanned the restaurant. "Is this all right?" he asked solicitously.

"Yes, it's lovely," Lauren assured him. My God, she thought, they sounded as if they were on their first date. Mercifully, the waiter appeared to take their drink order.

"Good evening, Mr. Caldwell." The pleasant-looking young man made a valiant attempt at a smile, but it came out with a twitch; he was obviously very hassled. "Would you care for a drink?" He turned his shaky smile on Lauren, and a sudden interest focused his glazed eyes as they moved over her.

Once again, she had the distinct feeling that she was being measured against Jason's previous dinner partners. She didn't know which bothered her more: the fact that everyone assumed that she was Jason's date, or the thought of Jason with other women.

Before she was able to come up with an answer, Jason's polite inquiry broke in. "What would you like, Lauren?"

"A Campari and soda."

"A Campari and soda for the lady," Jason ordered, "and an extra-dry vodka martini for me."

The waiter hurried away to fill their order, scribbling frantically as he went. He left a definite void in the conversation that neither of them seemed able to fill. Jason moved his silverware further to the right. Lauren reached over and picked up one of the menus.

"The bay scallops are excellent," Jason offered helpfully. "So is the Portuguese-style squid."

Lauren suppressed a wry smile. She was beginning to realize the absurdity of their situation. They'd known each other for years, yet here they were acting as if this were the first time they'd gone out to dinner together. Then it hit her: since their relationship had changed so completely, in a very real sense it *was* like the first time.

"What's the specialty of the house?" she asked, cringing inside as she did.

Jason nodded in the direction of the hundred-gallon tank. "Lobster."

Glancing over at the tank, Lauren was relieved to see their waiter snaking his way through the crowded tables. He was moving so quickly, she was amazed that he didn't spill a drop of their drinks. The tray he was balancing seemed to be an extension of his hand. But he did let out a sigh of relief when he set their miraculously intact drinks down in front of them. "Are you ready to order?" he asked a bit breathlessly.

"We'll have our drinks first," Jason said before turning abruptly to Lauren. "Is that all right?"

My God, why was he being so polite? she wondered. It wasn't like him at all. Instead of telling her what to do, he was actually asking her opinion. She nodded in agreement.

"Mr. Caldwell, it might be better to order," the waiter suggested. "They're all backed up in the kitchen. If I put your order in now, there'll still be a half-hour wait."

"Do you mind ordering now, Lauren?"

"Not at all." She quickly scanned the menu she was still holding. "I'll have a cup of the New England clam chowder, a salad with the house dressing and . . . a lobster."

"Lobster?" One of Jason's slanted black eyebrows went up. He'd remembered that when she was a young girl he could never get her to eat lobster.

But Lauren wasn't an unsophisticated young girl any longer. She looked up at the waiter. "I'd like my lobster steamed instead of boiled, please."

"I'll have exactly the same," Jason ordered, trying not to show his amusement. It was clear that she was trying to prove to him how grown-up she was now. He wondered what she would say if he told her how long he'd waited for her to grow up.

"What would you like to drink with that?" asked the waiter, scribbling away. With a wave of his hand and a half smile, Jason deferred the choice to Lauren.

"White wine." She slid Jason what she hoped was a woman-of-the-world look. "A Soave would be nice. What do you think?"

"Soave would be perfect," he allowed with a wry smile. As the waiter rushed off again, Jason picked up his cocktail glass and lifted it in a toast.

As always, Lauren was surprised that such a powerfully built man could have such beautiful, sensitive hands. But as she raised her glass to meet his, she tried not to remember just how powerful his hands could be.

"Welcome home, Lauren," Jason toasted. His voice had turned soft and deep, and when his eyes met hers, she was stunned by the warmth suffusing them. "I'm very glad you're home."

Jason saw the surprised look in Lauren's eyes turn instantly to one of pleasure. "Thank you, Jason," she murmured with a glowing smile. Her lips remained parted, soft and vulnerable, downright edible. He felt a growing hunger inside him that had nothing to do with food.

Tearing his gaze away, Jason took a careful sip of his vodka martini; when he spoke, his tone was merely polite again. "I know it's made all the difference to Clarissa. You've done more for her in a week than the doctors have in months."

Lauren paused as she was about to taste her aperitif, and she stared at Jason over the rim of her glass. Had she imagined the softness in his tone, the warmth in his eyes? She was sure that she hadn't. Yet, typically, just as she opened up to him, he closed down on her. Taking a slow, thoughtful sip of her drink, she set her glass back on the table. "Why do you always do that to me?"

"Do...what?" He looked genuinely confused.

"First, you—" she began, then stopped because the waiter had suddenly materialized beside their table carrying their salads and a bottle of Soave.

"I thought you'd like to have your wine now," he said, pulling a corkscrew out of his back pocket. "Your lobsters will be ready in twenty minutes."

"That's perfect," said Jason. He casually picked up his original conversation with Lauren while the waiter opened the bottle of wine. "I'm delighted that Clarissa is doing so well, thanks to you."

"All I did was keep her company and let her talk out her feelings," Lauren returned in the same tone. "And I got in touch with Evan. He's promised to come down next weekend."

"Yes, you told me."

"That's right," she remembered out loud. She had told Jason all about Clarissa in the car in order to cover up the tense silence between them while they drove from Truro to P'town. "I was thinking of giving a little dinner party next Saturday to encourage her to come downstairs. Is that all right with you?"

"I think it's a great idea," Jason said before sampling the wine the waiter had just poured for him. He nodded his approval, and the waiter filled both their glasses, then went again. Sitting back in his chair, Jason watched Lauren as she pretended a sudden interest in the view of the harbor. "What were you going to say before?"

"It wasn't important." Lauren had decided not to go into it. She knew that she would expose her feelings, only to end up with one of his sarcastic replies for her effort. She reached for her glass and sipped her aperitif. Jason took a long, hard pull on his drink.

"I've been meaning to ask *you* something," he said unexpectedly, staring into the transparent depths of his martini.

"What?"

"Something you said the other day has been bothering me." He twirled the stem of his cocktail glass between his long, sensitive fingers. "I still can't figure out what you meant by it."

"What did I say?"

He looked up at her then, his eyes dark and intense. "You said that if it hadn't been for me, you would never have married Carter."

"Oh, that," she murmured.

That had been something she'd blurted out because he'd upset her; something that, until that moment, she'd been unaware of herself. She'd thought about it quite a bit since and had finally faced the fact that the real reason she'd married Carter was to run away from Jason and the frightening feelings he'd aroused in her that night. She'd been unable to deal with those feelings then. She wasn't so sure she could deal with them even now. But there was one thing she did know: she certainly couldn't admit the truth to him.

"What exactly did you mean by that?" Jason persisted, taking another hard swallow of his drink.

"It was just something I said in anger," she replied evasively. The expression on his face made it clear he wasn't going to let her get out of it that easily. She tried shrugging it off. "Maybe if you'd given me more freedom, the chance to date Carter and see for myself what kind of a man he was, I wouldn't have married him."

"How long were you married?" He'd managed to keep his voice casual, but the image of Lauren in bed with Carter twisted slowly inside him like a dull-edged knife.

"A little over a year." She sent him a wry look. "You were right, of course. We weren't married six months before he started running around."

"I hate to say I told you so, but I told you so," he drawled, and was surprised to find that it gave him precious little satisfaction. He made himself a promise that if he ever saw Carter again, he'd break his handsome neck for him. "I knew that with a type like Carter it was only a matter of time before he left you."

Lauren sat up proudly in her chair. "Carter didn't leave me, Jason, I left him. He would have been perfectly happy to keep our marriage going—as long as he was allowed his little adventures from time to time." She shook her head as though she still found that impossible to comprehend, and her long platinum hair swayed softly around her face. "Right up to the very end, he swore that the others meant nothing to him, that I was the only one he loved." A rueful smile flickered across her face. "Poor Carter."

"You're still in love with him," said Jason tightly.

"No. If I loved him, I would have fought to save our marriage." Reaching for the swizzle stick in the shape of an anchor, she stirred the remains of her Campari and soda slowly, absently. "I don't think I ever really loved him. Oh, I was infatuated with him all right... with his looks and charm, his wonderful sense of fun. *Everybody* is." She laughed, but it came out in brittle pieces.

Lauren finished her drink in one gulp, then stared thoughtfully into the empty glass. "I married Carter for all the wrong reasons. The failure of our marriage was as much my fault as his."

"Why do I get the feeling it wasn't quite as easy as you make it sound?" Jason asked bluntly.

"I never said it was easy," she murmured, memories darkening her eyes. "But I survived it, and I became my own woman in the process."

"Yes, I can see that." There was no sarcasm in his tone, though she'd expected it, and the look he gave her was one of pure admiration. It bothered her that his approval still meant so much to her.

"Have you met someone else?" he asked matter-of-factly. "I can't believe that you would be lonely for male companionship for long."

"Companionship?" she repeated, her voice hard. "That was the one thing that was never offered me. I preferred to decline what was."

"You sound very bitter about men," he said in a surprised tone. "That's not like you."

"No, I'm not bitter, just smarter." She smiled. He never knew that a smile could be so sad. "Though there are some things about men a woman should never have to learn about."

"Such as?"

"How charmingly they lie. How afraid they are to love," she recited, punctuating each accusation with a careless shrug that sought to belie the pain deep in her eyes. "And how very easy it is for them to slip from another woman's bed into yours."

"Not all men are like that, Lauren," Jason insisted, leaning across the table toward her. He longed to reach out and take her in his arms, to hold her until all her pain went away and prove to her how much a man could love one woman. But he knew that in a moment of jealous rage he'd hurt her so deeply, she now despised him as much as any of those other men who'd tried to use her.

Jason sank back against his chair, into the safe pose he'd always adopted with her. "You can't let one bad experience turn you off love for the rest of your life, Lauren."

Lauren stiffened automatically at the sound of Jason's legal-guardian tone. "Music is my life right now," she told him coolly, trying to appear sophisticated but not doing a very good job of it. "Music is the only thing you can depend on, that will always sustain you—isn't that what you always tried to teach me, Jason?''

"I was wrong," he admitted bluntly. If he'd learned anything in the last four years, it was just how wrong he'd been. "All your accomplishments are empty, meaningless, unless you have someone to share them with."

"That's pretty funny coming from you," Lauren shot back accusingly before she could stop herself. "*You've* never needed anyone to share things with."

"No, of course not," he drawled with a twisted smile, "but you don't want to end up like me, do you?"

Lauren was completely thrown by Jason's startling admission; before she could recover, the waiter had materialized beside them.

"Here's your clam chowder," he announced with a frazzled smile. He set the steaming bowls of soup before them, sending chunks of clams surfing over chowder waves. "I'll have your lobsters for you in a few minutes," he tossed over his shoulder as he hurried off again.

"Jason, I'd always—"

"This is absolutely the best clam chowder in P'town," Jason declared, reaching for his spoon.

But Lauren wasn't about to let him change the subject. He'd just exposed a side of himself she'd never seen before, had never even dreamed existed, and she wanted to see more. "I'd always thought you preferred living alone, Jason."

"Really?" His tone was one of detached amusement. "But I've only been living alone for the past four years."

"No, uh, that's not what I meant." Lauren shook out her linen napkin and spread it on her lap in an attempt to hide the sudden, strange embarrassment she felt. "I was talking about needing someone... to love."

"So was I," he muttered cryptically as he attacked his clam chowder. "You really should eat that while it's hot," he added, nodding in the direction of her soup.

Lauren knew Jason well enough not to attempt to reopen the conversation once he'd closed it. Picking up her spoon, she dug into the thick, creamy chowder.

Seven

From then until the end of the meal, they both kept to the safer subject of music. Lauren discussed the problems she was still having with the *Emperor* Concerto. Jason talked about his music publishing house, a pet project of his to help new composers, that was just beginning to break even.

At the end of the meal, which was every bit as delicious as he'd predicted, Jason suggested having their after-dinner drinks upstairs in the more relaxed atmosphere of the café dansant. To her surprise, Lauren found that she was reluctant for the evening to end. She agreed.

The café dansant, which sprawled over what was actually the roof of the building, was still enclosed in its protective winter covering of glass. In keeping with the maritime theme of the establishment, the front section was shaped like the deck of a ship; jutting out over the bay, it hung suspended between water and sky. Café tables sporting colorful striped umbrellas circled the dance floor, and the chairs were a plushier version of deck chairs. The multicolored lanterns strung in midair twinkled like the stars that were visible through the glass dome, adding to the illusion of being aboard a luxury cruise ship.

Music from a solo violin greeted them as they went in, and Lauren noticed the strolling violinist regaling a starry-eyed couple with a lushly romantic show tune. The hostess had barely seated them and taken their order when the short, chubby violinist, launching into another lush melody, came strolling over to their table on surprisingly dainty feet. From the gleam in his moist, soulful eyes, it was clear he'd assumed they were a starry-eyed couple, too.

Lauren squirmed in her seat. Knowing how Jason abhorred schmaltzy music, she felt sure he'd encourage the strolling violinist to keep on strolling. Instead he leaned across the table toward her and asked softly, "Is there anything in particular you'd like to hear?"

Stunned, all Lauren could do was shake her head.

"Do you know Ravel's Tzigane?" Jason asked the violinist.

"Certainly." The violinist beamed, clearly delighted that someone had finally asked him to play a virtuoso piece. Drawing himself up proudly, he tore into the gypsy Tzigane as if he'd been waiting all his life to play it. Eyes closed, emotion working the muscles of his face, he drew such heartfelt sounds from his instrument that everyone in the café turned to look at Jason and Lauren's table.

Lauren cringed inside as she found herself and Jason the objects of much speculation. She just knew that everyone assumed they were lovers. She wished one of the waitresses would appear with their drinks so she would have something to do with her hands. Clenching them in her lap, she slid Jason a look to see how he was reacting to all the attention. He seemed oblivious to everyone but her.

The flickering light from the lanterns softened the craggy lines of his face, made his dark eyes glow with a disturbing intensity. As the wild gypsy music swirled around them, Lauren found herself wondering what it would be like if Jason were her lover. Something quickened inside her, and she reexperienced the sensation of his arms around her, the burning crush of his mouth. Her pulse speeded up when she visualized how the evening would end if they were lovers.

As if he'd read her mind or was sharing the same thoughts, Jason's lips parted. It was the subtlest of movements, but Lauren felt the sensuality behind it, a hunger that frightened and excited her at the same time. Unconsciously, her own lips parted in response. His eyes locked with hers, questioning, seeking to find some answer. A burst of applause went up as the violinist finished the piece with a flourish, startling Lauren back to herself.

"That was wonderful," Jason said. Slowly he turned his head to look up at the musician.

"My pleasure, sir." Pulling a handkerchief out of his pocket, he first patted his violin and then his cheek, both glistening with sweat from the physical and emotional exertion of playing.

As the waitress set their Drambuies down before them, Lauren watched Jason question the violinist about his musical background. There was no condescension in his tone; he seemed genuinely interested.

Lauren was grateful for the chance to get herself back under control. She wondered whether she'd imagined what had just passed between them. Something told her that she hadn't.

Gratified by the attention and appreciation he was unaccustomed to receiving, the musician answered Jason's questions willingly. When Jason slipped him a twenty-dollar bill, he thanked him effusively and offered to play another selection, but the four-piece salsa band, back from their break, was launching into the opening number.

The strong Latin beat matched Lauren's still-erratically beating pulse as she reached for her drink. Though she wasn't looking at Jason, she could feel him studying her with the same questioning intensity.

Sipping her liqueur, she glanced out at the harbor. The beam of a searchlight was gliding languorously over the dark waters, illuminating the yachts and sailboats moored side by side with fishing trawlers. Myriad stars glittered like diamonds in the black velvet sky, and there was a hazy ring around the moon.

"This certainly is a very romantic place," Lauren said lightly, hoping to relieve the sudden tension between them. She managed a mischievous grin. "Is this where you usually bring your lady friends?"

Jason took a long, slow swallow of his drink. "As a matter of fact, this is the first time I've been up here myself."

"But you do eat here a lot," she insisted. "Everyone knows you, and I had the feeling that they were all comparing me to your other... to your usual dates."

"Really?" He slid her an amused smile. "But I've never brought a woman here before."

Lauren was unable to conceal her surprise, and it took her a moment to recover. "Maybe *that's* why they were staring at me," she murmured as if to herself.

"I have so many social obligations when I'm in Boston," he explained. "I've always preferred to eat here alone."

It suddenly occurred to Lauren that in all the years she'd known him, Jason had never brought one of his women to the Cape. She wondered, as she took another sip of her drink, whether there was a special woman waiting for him in Boston right now, and if she were the reason he'd been spending so much time there.

"Is there a special lady in your life right now?" she blurted out before she could stop herself.

He smiled wryly. "A special lady?" That was all he would say.

"Well, since I saw you last, I've been married and divorced and I . . . I just wondered what's been happening with you," she rattled on. She was sorry she'd brought up the subject now, but not knowing how to get out of it gracefully, she went on. "Are you planning any change in your, uh, marital status?" she finished lamely.

"Me, get married?" he muttered incredulously. "Who the hell could put up with me?"

"I'm sure there are plenty of women who would be only too delighted to try, if you gave them half the chance." Lauren was the first one to admit that Jason wasn't the easiest man to get along with at times, but at least he wasn't a phony like most of the men she'd met in New York. "You've got a great deal to offer a woman, Jason."

"Really?" One slanted black eyebrow went up. "Like what?"

"Well, you're talented and successful and . . . and attractive, and you—"

"Attractive?" He laughed harshly. "You call this face attractive?"

Lauren looked at Jason wonderingly. The flickering lights played up the uneven but startlingly dramatic lines of his face, his dark, intense eyes and sensual mouth. It seemed to her that he'd never looked more attractive. "Yes, attractive."

Cradling the snifter in one long, beautiful hand, Jason leaned back in his chair. "Define your terms," he said with detached amusement. "When you say attractive, you mean like Carter?"

"No, not like Carter," she admitted honestly. "Carter is almost absurdly handsome."

"So he is," he shot back. "And let's not forget unconventional and full of fun." Everything I'm not, Jason thought miserably.

Lauren was amazed that Jason had remembered her exact description of Carter. She watched his fingers tighten around his glass as he lifted it to lips that had narrowed into a hard line. She never knew that Jason was so sensitive about his looks, or that he even cared about such things. There were a lot of things about him she didn't know, Lauren realized, but she was learning fast. She leaned across the table toward him. "Jason, believe me, in many ways you're a much more attractive man than Carter."

"Really?" he drawled sarcastically.

"But you *are,*" Lauren insisted, though she'd only just realized it herself. "You're much more . . ." *Virile,* she thought, to her own amazement, *sensual, exciting.* " . . . Intelligent, capable, dependable," she said. "Perfect husband material."

"Thank you, I think."

"And I'm sure, as an eligible bachelor, you'd have your pick of eager candidates."

"I've met my share," he admitted with a disinterested shrug. "But they were usually after one thing, and I was after another." He met her eyes with a level stare. "*I* have no intention of marrying for the wrong reasons."

Lauren let that one go by; she was too intrigued with uncovering a side of Jason she'd never known to bother about his little dig at her. She held his gaze unflinchingly. "But what if you fall in love?"

"Being able to love is a talent...like playing the piano," he said wryly. "Some people have it, and some people don't. I don't."

"You can achieve anything if you want it badly enough," she reminded him. "Isn't that what you used to teach me?"

"You know what they say," he tossed back with a twisted smile. "Those who can, do. Those who can't, teach."

Lauren was shocked by the utter futility in Jason's voice. She suddenly knew the reason why, as a young girl, she'd found his eyes so scary: a kind of despair of ever being loved darkened them. She longed to reach out to him, to tell him how much she'd always loved him, but she knew he would only react sarcastically. She was also beginning to realize how much pain was buried behind his sardonic facade. She wondered who had hurt him so deeply that he refused to let himself love again. And suddenly, she had to know.

He'd been sipping his drink and staring—somewhat wistfully, Lauren thought—at the starry-eyed couple she'd noticed when they first came in. They were dancing to the sensuous strains of a bossa nova, oblivious to everything around them, utterly lost in each other's arms. She couldn't help feeling a bit wistful herself.

"Jason?" She had to raise her voice over the music to get his attention. "Have you ever been in love?"

He slanted her one of his long looks, the kind that sought to decipher what was going on in her mind without giving away anything about himself. "What?"

"Well, I've told you all about my romantic trials and tribulations," she said lightly. "And I suddenly realized that in spite of all the years we've lived together, there's so much about you I don't know."

"I didn't know you were interested," he told his drink.

"I am," Lauren returned sincerely but with more emotion than she'd intended. "*Have* you ever been in love?"

He continued to stare into the amber depths of his glass. A strange smile tugged at the corners of his mouth. That was all the answer he would give her.

"I don't mean an infatuation," Lauren persisted, "or a physical attraction. I mean really in love."

Jason looked up at Lauren, and his breath caught. In the flickering light, her eyes were like the sea struck by moonlight, silvery green. "Once," he found himself admitting. "Only once."

"Did you love her very much?"

"Too much."

The semidarkness, the soft, sensuous strains of the bossa nova drifted around them, added to the strange new intimacy between them and gave Lauren the courage to go on. "What happened?"

"With my inimitable charm and personality, what could happen?" He shrugged fatalistically. "I screwed it up."

"And what about the woman?" She leaned across the table toward him, lamplight sliding and shimmering over her silk dress. "Did she love you?"

Jason searched Lauren's face intently for a moment, hoping to find the answer there. "I'm not sure," he had to admit finally. "I think she might have if..." His voice broke off.

"If?"

"It's getting late," Jason announced abruptly. "I think we should be heading home." Turning in his chair, he searched for their waitress, then signaled to her to bring him the check. When he turned back to Lauren, a sardonic smile tugged at his mouth. "Maybe I'll tell you all about it someday."

"Clarissa, has Jason ever been engaged?" Lauren asked matter-of-factly as she positioned the deck chair to catch the few rays of sun that managed to reach the porch. She had an unobstructed view of the green-gray ocean stretching clear to the horizon.

"Jason, engaged?" Clarissa looked up from the colorfully wrapped present Lauren had just given her to celebrate her first day out of bed since the operation. "No, never."

Lauren hesitated as she was about to sit down next to her aunt. "Well, he must have come close at least once."

"Not that I know of," Clarissa replied, tearing the wrapping off as eagerly as a child. "Jason was always a loner. As a young man, he was totally absorbed by his music and . . . oh, Laurie!" she cried when the gift was revealed to her. "These are those simply scrumptious French chocolates. You know that's my greatest weakness. How can I ever thank you?"

"By enjoying them." With a warm smile, Lauren plopped down onto the chair. She was delighted to see Clarissa acting like her old self again, but she was eager to get back to the subject of Jason. It was a subject that had been filling her thoughts since their dinner together. "Well, what about later on, after Jason gave up the piano and took over Caldwell Enterprises?"

"As you know, Jason spends a good deal of time in Boston," Clarissa said, peeling the gold foil off an almond-topped bonbon, "and there have been rumors from time to time, but . . ." She let out a moan of sheer delight as she popped the hand-dipped chocolate into her mouth. "Simply sinfully scrumptious," she groaned around the melting bonbon.

"What kind of rumors?"

"What?" Clarissa mumbled distractedly, lost in the kind of ecstasy only a confirmed chocolate addict could appreciate.

"You were saying that there have been rumors about Jason's love life," Lauren prompted. "What kind of rumors?"

"Just that Jason was seeing some woman or other, but I don't think that any of them meant very much to him. Here." Holding the box up, she offered Lauren a chocolate. "Have one."

"But there must have been one special woman," Lauren persisted.

"I don't believe so. If there had been, I'm sure Jason would have brought her home to meet his family." She shoved the box of chocolates practically under

Lauren's nose. "Laurie, you simply must try one of these."

"No, thanks," Lauren declined, content to experience her aunt's enjoyment vicariously. "I bought those for you. You can afford all those calories."

"If you insist," Clarissa returned gaily as she began peeling the gold foil off another bonbon.

Lauren was deeply disappointed at not finding out who the woman was that Jason had been in love with—was, perhaps, still in love with. Sinking back in the deck chair, she watched the sea gulls picking raucously through the gleaming strands of seaweed the tide had tossed up onto the sand.

"*I* was engaged to be married once," Clarissa said unexpectedly. "Did I ever tell you?"

"No," Lauren said, surprised. "You didn't."

"When I was twenty-nine. Everyone, including myself, was already resigned to my being an old maid, as they were called in my day." She popped the second chocolate into her mouth, then pushed it into one corner with her tongue so she could slowly savor it while she went on talking. "I wasn't much to look at even then. Laura was the beauty in the family, and—"

"Clarissa, you've got to stop putting yourself down," Lauren cut in. "You're a lovely woman and a wonderful one."

"*You* think so, Laurie, because you love me," she returned gratefully. "Anyway, I met this very nice man at one of the church socials. He wasn't much to look at, either, but he was so kind and sensitive. And he really cared about me." A baffled smile played on her thin lips as if she still found that difficult to believe. "And I cared very much for him."

"What happened?"

"We'd already announced our engagement when father had his stroke. I postponed the wedding so I could take care of him." She paused and slowly replaced the cover on the box of chocolates. "I'd thought it would only be for a few months. Who could have known that he'd linger on in that state for over three years?" She paused again as the memory swept over her, clouding her eyes. "I really couldn't blame Robert for not waiting."

"But what about your father's wife, Jason's mother?" Lauren asked indignantly. "Couldn't she take care of him?"

"Margot?" An uncharacteristically bitter laugh escaped her. "She could barely take care of herself. I was the one who ran the house even then."

"What was she like?" Unable to conceal her eagerness any longer, Lauren sat up in her chair. "I can't remember Jason ever talking about his mother."

"Oh, she was very beautiful. As exquisite as a porcelain doll." There was no envy in Clarissa's tone, only a kind of awed respect. "She was the most flighty woman I've ever seen. Frivolous, without a thought in her head, and very flirtatious. The kind of woman most men find so appealing."

"Not anymore, I hope," Lauren couldn't help interjecting. She wondered whether Jason would find that type of woman appealing. Somehow, she was sure that he wouldn't.

"There was something about Margot that made you want to protect her," Clarissa continued, setting the box of candy on the wicker table separating their chairs. "She knew just how to get everyone to do exactly what she wanted, but she did it with such grace and charm you simply couldn't dislike her." Bending over, Clarissa lifted the rag doll out of the wicker sewing basket lying at her feet. "I'll never forget the first time I saw Margot, when she came to this house with Jason. She'd lost her husband barely six months earlier, and—"

"Jason's father?" Lauren interrupted, becoming more intrigued by the minute. Once again, she realized how little she knew about Jason's past, how much she wanted to know about it.

"Yes." She continued searching through an assortment of needles for the one she needed. "He was a marine. Very gung ho, I understand." Her voice lowered in mournful respect, though she had never known him. "He was killed in action in Korea."

"How old was Jason?"

"Only eight years old, but I'll never forget it." She paused as she was about to thread a large upholstery needle. The vividness of the memory caused her to sit up and lean toward Lauren. "He was like a little man. He took care of his mother instead of the other way around. She depended on him for everything. I was only eighteen at the time, but I thought it was very strange."

"I would think so," Lauren agreed under her breath.

"Naturally, once she married Father and found a grown-up protector, she no longer needed Jason." Sitting back in her chair, Clarissa finished threading the needle. "At least, that's the impression I had. I always thought she neglected him shamefully. And then when Evan was born the following year, poor Jason was pushed even further into the background."

"Then she was close to Evan?"

"Oh, she adored him. But it was as though he were a live doll that she enjoyed playing with and showing off. *I'm* the one who actually took care of Evan. I suppose that's why I've always been so attached to him." An apologetic smile curved her lips. "I tried to get close to Jason, but even as a little boy he was so proud and self-sufficient. Maybe if I'd tried a little harder..." Her voice trailed off regretfully, and she began sewing on the shiny black button that matched the doll's other eye.

"Where is Jason's mother now?" Lauren asked; she'd never seen or heard from the woman the whole time she was living with the Caldwells.

"After Father died, Margot remarried—less than three months after. The family was scandalized." A disapproving frown creased Clarissa's high, pale forehead. "She obviously had... known the man while Father was still alive." She slanted her niece a look as pointed as her needle and made sure Lauren had gotten her meaning before she went on. "The last we heard, she'd moved to England with her new husband."

For a long moment Lauren stared at the brooding sand dunes rippling with beach grass. "No wonder Jason has never talked about any of this."

"I'll tell you another thing I'm sure Jason has never told you," Clarissa said impulsively. "But you must promise me you'll never tell him that I did."

"I promise." Pulling her long legs up, Lauren tucked them under her and leaned expectantly toward Clarissa. Her needle poised in midair, Clarissa hesitated, making Lauren wonder what her aunt's mysterious revelation could be. Was she finally going to reveal the identity of the only woman Jason had ever loved?

"Jason was just beginning to make a name for himself as a concert pianist when Father had his stroke," Clarissa went on, every word as precise as her stitches. "Music was the only thing Jason cared about then, but someone had to take over Caldwell Enterprises. Evan was too young, and it was obvious even then he had no head for business. And Jason had always felt indebted to Father for adopting him." With a heavy sigh, she finished making a double knot, then clipped the thread. "That's why Jason gave up his dream of being a concert pianist, Laurie. As head of the family, he's made himself responsible for everyone ever since."

"I'd always wondered why Jason gave up playing the piano when he loves music so much," Lauren murmured, unexpected tears misting her eyes. She was sure she would have been incapable of such a sacrifice. "No wonder he's so bitter."

"That's why we have to make allowances for Jason's moods," Clarissa said. "I know better than anyone how difficult he can be at times, but there aren't too many men like him around these days."

Lauren was beginning to come to the same conclusion. Blinking back the tears, she turned to look out at the ocean, but not in time to hide her reaction from her aunt.

"You still love Jason very much, don't you, Laurie?"

"Yes, Clarissa," Lauren admitted shakily, "very much."

Eight

As Lauren launched into the most passionate section of the sonata, shaking out trills and broken chords, gliding across interlocking octaves, a sudden cramp in her right arm made her gasp with pain, causing her to hit several wrong notes. Lifting her contorted fingers off the keys, she shook her arm slowly, trying to loosen the knotted-up muscles. When that didn't help, she carefully kneaded her forearm with her left hand until the pain and tension had eased and she was able to move her fingers normally again.

Her hands were shaking when she rested them on the keyboard once more. That was the second time in half an hour that the muscles in her arm had cramped. Along with loss of memory, sudden cramping was one of a pianist's most dreaded fears. The worst thing about it was that she couldn't understand why it was happening. She'd practiced Schumann's Sonata in F Minor countless times, and she was used to playing pieces that were far more demanding technically without having any physical problems. Using the relaxation techniques Jason had taught her...

Lauren's hands slid off the keyboard into her lap. That was it, she realized; Jason was the problem.

Since the night they'd gone out to dinner together, there had been a subtle change in their relationship. Jason no longer went out of his way to avoid her; during the past week he hadn't spent a single night in Boston. Instead, after the two of them had dinner with Clarissa, they would spend the rest of the evening together.

The night before, Lauren had finally had the courage to play the *Emperor* Concerto for Jason, going over the sections she still wasn't satisfied with, and he'd given her some excellent suggestions. But most evenings they just lounged about the living room in front of a crackling fire, Killer curled up at Jason's feet, and talked.

Lauren had to admit that she thoroughly enjoyed their talks; she hadn't realized how much she'd missed them. She had yet to meet a man who possessed Jason's incisive intelligence and instinctive understanding, or one who enjoyed, rather than resented, listening to a woman express her own opinions. It occurred to her belatedly that if he hadn't practically forced her to think for herself as a teenager, she probably wouldn't have had any opinions to express.

Although their conversations were interesting and spirited, Lauren was beginning to get the feeling that they were using them as a way of not really dealing with one another. There were too many awkward pauses and long, cryptic looks, and always that underlying tension between them. Several times, after a particularly heavy pause, she sensed that Jason was on the verge of telling her what was really going on inside him, but he never did.

And just the other night, as he was helping her out of her chair, she had felt his hand tremble as it closed around hers. There was a moment, when she looked up into his eyes, that she was sure he was going to kiss her. It still bothered Lauren to remember how much she'd wanted Jason to kiss her, how disappointed she'd been that he hadn't.

Every day she swore to herself that that night she would finally confront him. She certainly couldn't let things go on the way they were. She had to know whether she was misinterpreting his signals and if the emotional and sensual tension she felt were merely a projection of her own desires. But every night something inside her made her hold back.

She told herself that she didn't want to spoil the fragile new relationship that had developed between them and risk putting an end to the lovely evenings they shared. As it was, she was always sorry when their evenings together ended, and she found herself looking forward to the next one much too eagerly.

Lauren warned herself against what she was allowing to happen to her, but it didn't do any good. She could no longer deny the love she felt for Jason. It had been the center of her life for too many years, had grown as she'd grown—from a girlish adulation to a woman's consuming passion. Night after restless night, he filled her dreams. She longed to tell him how much she loved and wanted him, but the words wouldn't come. She finally decided to tell him in the only way she knew how.

Moving resolutely back to the keyboard, Lauren's fingers plunged into the opening bars of the sonata. Something wrenched inside her as it always did when she played those notes. The Sonata No. 3 in F Minor was a desperate cry of passion that Robert Schumann had composed when he'd lost all hope of marrying his great and only love, Clara Wieck.

Convinced that the penniless composer would ruin his daughter's successful career as a concert pianist, Clara's father had forbidden her to see him again. Her mail censored, her every move watched, unable to communicate with Robert in private, Clara did so in public.

Having learned that he planned to attend her next piano recital, she deliberately played the sonata he'd dedicated to her, to convey the depth of her love for him and her desire to be his wife in spite of the obstacles that separated them. Schumann recognized her musical declaration of love. Theirs proved to be an idyllic marriage, Clara's love lasting long after Robert's tragic death.

Lauren had deliberately chosen to play the sonata for Jason after the dinner party she was giving that evening to celebrate Evan's homecoming. As her fingers glided over the keys, she gave herself up to the lush, romantic sweep of the music. Jason himself had told her the story behind Schumann's passionate composition and how Clara had chosen to prove her love for him. Lauren wondered whether Jason would get her musical message and what his reaction would be. Another sudden spasm in Lauren's arm sent pain shooting down to her fingertips and splintered the chord she was playing into dissonance.

What if that happened while she was performing later, she thought anxiously. There was no doubt in her mind now that her fear of being rejected by Jason was responsible for her cramping. As she rubbed her arm and slowly flexed her fingers she began to have second thoughts about playing the sonata.

"Are you all right?" Jason asked from across the room, his voice tight with concern.

Lauren gasped soundlessly, staring at him as though the sheer power of her thoughts had caused him to materialize out of nowhere. She managed a quick nod.

He strode toward her purposefully. "What's wrong with your arm?"

"Oh, nothing." She dropped her arm to her side.

"Cramped?" Pushing the metronome and stopwatch to one side, Jason placed the manila folder he was carrying on top of the piano. "Let me see." He held out his hand.

"It's nothing, really."

"Let me see," he grated.

Lauren lifted her arm reluctantly. Holding her wrist carefully in one hand, Jason pushed her long, flowing sleeve up to her shoulder. Lauren suddenly realized she was sitting there in her robe with nothing on underneath except the flimsiest of panties. As if prompted by her thoughts again, Jason's eyes moved over her paisley silk robe; he quickly came to the same realization.

"I brought you those charts we talked about the other night," he said tightly, his eyes shifting to the folder.

"Charts?"

"The fingering charts," he reminded her while he began to feel and test every muscle in her forearm, sending tiny shivers up her spine. "The fingering you're

using in the opening cadenza of the *Emperor* is marvel-
ous . . .''

Lauren suppressed a wry smile. Talk about marvel-
ous fingering! What he was doing to her arm felt so delicious, it had to be illegal.

'' . . . But I don't think you should risk it at the start
of a concerto, not until you get used to the sound of the
piano and the hall.'' Lauren stiffened as Jason kneaded
the sensitive flesh of her upper arm. ''Did I hurt you?''

''No,'' she breathed.

His hand moved to her shoulder, pulling the
bunched-up fabric along with it. ''Does your arm cramp
up like this often?''

''No, never.''

''You've either forgotten everything I taught you,''
he said dryly, ''and you're doing something wrong
physically, or it's psychological.''

''I think it's just tension,'' Lauren admitted with
difficulty. ''I always get anxious before—oh!'' She
gasped with pain as Jason's fingers sank into the most
sensitive part of her shoulder.

''You sure as hell are tense,'' he muttered. ''This
muscle is as hard as a rock.'' His hand released the sore
spot to slide down her arm, the silky sleeve tumbling
down after it. Moving abruptly behind the piano bench,
he placed both hands on her shoulders. Lauren jumped
as she felt the unexpected warmth of his touch through
the delicate fabric of her robe. ''I'm not going to hurt
you,'' he promised softly. ''Take a deep breath and try
to relax.''

Lauren drew in a long, deep breath, but as Jason's
hands moved over her back her breath came out in ragged pieces. She took another deep breath, counting to
ten in an effort to hold it in. Placing his thumbs on

either side of her spine, he moved slowly, searchingly, down the length of it. She felt as if her spine would melt under the warm pressure. The breath rushed out of her.

His thumbs came to a sudden halt. "Here's what the problem is."

Lauren knew what the problem was; she just didn't have the nerve to tell him.

"Right here." His thumbs rubbed up and down on the spot, sending a tiny shiver through her. "This is what's making your arm cramp. Your back is out from all that tension." He came around the piano bench to face her. "I can help you with that," he offered. "I don't know how serious it is. You may need a chiropractor, but I can take care of it temporarily."

She looked up at him as he stood towering over her. "What do you mean, take care of it?"

"With a massage."

"That's what I thought you meant," she murmured.

"It's just a matter of breaking up the tension that's knotting up the muscles in your back and constricting the flow of blood to your arm," he explained matter-of-factly. "At least you'll be able to perform tonight without any problems."

Lauren was about to assure Jason that she didn't need a massage, but her fear of cramping during the performance made her change her mind. She didn't want anything to go wrong tonight. She wanted to perform more brilliantly than she ever had in her life. "All right," she agreed. Bending over from the waist, she folded her arms on top of the piano and rested her forehead on them.

"I don't think that's going to work," said Jason wryly. "You really should lie down."

Lauren's head shot up. "Lie down?"

"Your spine should be in a flat position."

"Of course," she replied airily, as though she were supremely conversant with the rituals of a massage. She slid out from behind the piano, causing her robe to fall open and reveal a long expanse of leg. Quickly tugging the front of her robe closed, she added, "But I don't think we have enough time."

"It's just past five. We're not expecting anyone until seven."

Lauren had known that there was plenty of time—that's why she'd impulsively postponed her shower to practice the sonata—but the situation was becoming more complicated than she'd anticipated.

"This won't take very long," Jason assured her. "It's just a simple massage."

"All right, where do you want me to, uh, lie down?" Turning away from him, she scanned the parlor. "The love seat isn't long enough. How about the rug in front of the fireplace?"

"You may find the floor under it a bit hard," he said, his tone a lesson in understatement. "I know my knees would."

"Well, where do you suggest?"

An ironic smile played on his lips. "How about the bed?"

"Oh, the bed. Sure." She tossed off a why-didn't-I-think-of-that-myself shrug as she started across the parlor to the bedroom. Her knees were shaking and her insides felt like jelly, but her pulse was beating hard and strong.

Sliding open the pocket doors, Lauren stepped resolutely into the bedroom ahead of Jason. She felt sure that her manner implied that nothing out of the ordinary was taking place. The sight of the bed, all soft and lacy, totally inviting, stopped her cold.

It's just a simple massage, she assured herself as she forced herself to cross to the bed; he's not going to make love to you. The knot in her stomach was beginning to rival the one in her back just at the thought. She wondered why she was afraid of something she wanted so desperately.

"Just lie down on your stomach and stretch out comfortably," Jason ordered, sounding as though he were instructing her on a particularly difficult passage of music. "Slip your arms out of the sleeves and leave the front of your robe open."

Lauren remembered that she was practically naked under her robe. Jason, realizing that she was unable to follow his instructions as long as he was looking at her, turned away. "Do you have any baby oil or some kind of lotion?"

"There should be some body lotion on top of the vanity," Lauren replied, lying facedown on the bed. She slid Jason a look over her shoulder. When she saw that he was standing with his back to her, she reached under herself to untie her belt and found that lying on top of it was not the easiest way to go about it. She had to wrestle the robe open, but she finally managed to pull her arms out of the sleeves without dislocating her shoulders, then spread out the front sections of the robe on either side of her. The antique-lace bedspread felt scratchy and cold against her skin.

"This should do it," she heard Jason say as he came toward the bed. Now that she could only hear him, Lauren was aware of a definite strain in his voice. Stretching out under the loose covering of the silk robe, she folded her hands on the pillow and rested her burning cheek on them.

From the corner of her eye, she saw Jason set the bottle of lotion down on the bed, propping it up against her hip. "Are you comfortable?" he asked while he quickly rolled up the sleeves of his flannel shirt.

"Yes," she breathed, trying not to stare at the play of muscles in his powerful arms, their sprinkling of coarse dark hair. Her heart slammed against her rib cage when he suddenly sat down on the bed next to her.

"I don't want to ruin your lovely bedspread," he explained as he bent over and started pulling off his shoes.

"My bedspread?"

"Well, I have to get up on the bed with you in order to apply the proper pressure to your back," he pointed out wryly.

"That's right," she said as if she knew what the procedure was and it had merely slipped her mind. She held her breath as he swung his long legs onto the bed; when he straddled her thighs, she stopped breathing altogether.

A tiny shiver went through Lauren when Jason's fingers slid unexpectedly under her hair to brush the long platinum strands off her neck and shoulders onto the pillow. Moving to the nape of her neck, they curled around the edge of her robe and pulled it down past her shoulders. When he shifted his weight to reach for the bottle of lotion, she felt the muscles of his thighs slide against hers.

Jason poured some lotion into his hands, then rubbed it slowly between his palms to warm it before applying it to her bare skin. "This smells just like your perfume."

"Yes." She was amazed that he would recognize the scent she wore. She didn't know that men were aware of such things. "White Shoulders."

"They sure are," he murmured thickly. With long, even strokes from the sides of her neck to the ends of her shoulders, he began rubbing the scented lotion into her skin.

"That's the name of the—oh!"

"I'm sorry if that hurt. I'm just trying to warm up your muscles, but you're so tense." His hands continued smoothing on the lotion with long, measured strokes. "Try to relax."

Lauren took a deep breath and willed her body to go limp, but the disturbing warmth of Jason's touch and the feeling of his strong thighs gripping hers weren't helping any. She felt the beginnings of a different kind of tension building inside her.

"What do you think is causing all this tension?" he asked while his fingers began to knead her flesh with a slow, rhythmic action. "Is something bothering you?"

"No," she assured him after only the slightest of pauses. She could hardly tell him that *he* was the cause, especially under those circumstances. "I guess I'm just tired."

Slowly, Jason increased the pressure, deepening the rhythmic movements, drawing all the pain and tension out of her knotted-up muscles. Her eyes fluttered closed. "Why are you so tired?" His voice was soft and deep, as soothing as his fingers. "Have you been having trouble sleeping?"

"Not really, I . . ." A ragged sigh escaped her as she gave herself up to the drugging warmth of his hands, the hypnotic sound of his voice.

"Then what's the problem?"

"I've been having the craziest dreams. Sometimes I wake up more tired than when I went to sleep."

"Yeah, dreams," he murmured, as though he knew exactly what she was talking about. His hands moved farther down her back, the robe sliding out of their way. With the heel of his hand, he began to slowly work the kinks out of the muscles under her shoulder blade. A delicious heaviness began to suffuse Lauren's body.

"You're probably bored and restless. After living in New York, the off-season Cape must seem pretty dull to you." His hands shifted to work their rough magic on her other shoulder blade. "Now that Clarissa's on her feet again, I'm sure you can't wait to get back to Fun City."

Adrift in a languorous daze, Lauren hadn't heard Jason's words clearly. The sarcasm in his tone broke through to her. Her eyes opened reluctantly. "What did you say?"

"Nothing," he grated. She felt his hands stiffen before they slid all the way down her back, pushing the robe out of their way impatiently. Lauren gasped as she felt the cool air on her heated skin, felt her own nakedness. With long, sensuous strokes, Jason's hands glided up her back again.

At first, Lauren was so completely thrown by the change in Jason's touch that she had no defense for it. She quickly found she didn't want one. Her eyes fluttered closed again. She felt her body begin to change also, to soften and swell under the hungry pull of his hands. An intense longing for him swept over her, sweeping away all doubts and fears. She ached to feel *his* skin under *her* hands, to feel him all over her. Her breath caught in her throat as his fingers traced the curves of her hips slowly, erotically; when she felt their feathery touch at the sides of her breasts, she had to bury her face in the pillow to stifle a moan.

Pulling his hands away abruptly, Jason sat back up on his heels. Lifting her head, Lauren slanted him a questioning look over her shoulder. She thought she caught a glimmer of perverse satisfaction in his eyes before he turned his face away. Leaning over, he reached for the bottle of lotion.

"Jason?" His name was more a plea than a question.

"I'm almost finished," he replied coolly while he poured out some more lotion. Carefully warming it in his palms, he turned back to her, his manner as impersonal as a professional masseur's.

Lauren's head sank down slowly on the pillow. Had she imagined the change in his touch? Had it been merely a projection of her own desires again?

Warm and moist, softly fragrant, Jason's hands settled on her lower back. "This is the spot where your back is out," he informed her evenly. Spreading his fingers, he placed his thumbs on either side of her spine. His handspan was so wide that his fingers curved around her waist. With growing pressure, he slowly rotated his thumbs, sending an ever-expanding circle of heat radiating outward. It seemed as if her spine were melting, all of the remaining tension slowly draining out of her.

Lauren let out a long, contented sigh as Jason ran his magical fingers all the way up her spine. She could feel his fingertips pressing down on each of her vertebrae as if they were keys on a piano, each note vibrating inside her, separate and complete. She sighed again. "You must have been a great pianist."

"What makes you say that?" asked Jason wryly, his fingers doing a quick glissando up her back.

"You have such a wide handspan," she murmured languorously, "and your fingering is fantastic."

"I'm glad all those years of practicing weren't totally wasted." His voice had its usual sardonic edge, but his touch was meltingly tender.

"I wish you would play for me sometime, Jason."

He pulled his hands away abruptly, and she almost cried out at the unexpected loss. Quickly reaching for her robe, which was bunched up around her hips, he drew it over her, the silky fabric shivering up her back. "Do you feel any better?"

"God, yes," she admitted with a grateful sigh, although she wished that he would go on touching her, that he would never stop touching her. "Thanks." Lauren had to stifle the impulse to roll over and brazenly offer Jason her breasts, which ached for the feel of him. If he said the word, she would have offered him all of her.

As if he'd somehow sensed her intense longing for him, Jason's thighs contracted against hers. Then, for an agonizingly long moment, he didn't so much as move a muscle. Lauren held her breath, her heart pounding inside her.

"Just lie there and rest for a few minutes," he ordered finally, his voice neutral. With a single fluid motion, he swung his leg over her and sat up on the edge of the bed.

Tears burning behind her eyes, Lauren raised her head and looked over at Jason. His profile was a proud, jagged silhouette against the dying sunlight filtering through the windows. Tension coiled the powerful muscles of his back.

Lauren's hands clenched into fists to keep from touching him; she was afraid that he didn't want her to touch him. "Jason, why..." she began, then choked on the question she'd been wanting to ask him for years: why won't you love me anymore? Instead she said, "Why won't you play for me?"

"I haven't played the piano since I gave up all hope of being a concert pianist, Lauren," he returned flatly, bending over to get his shoes. "You know that."

"You played for me once."

"Did I?" he asked while he slipped on his shoes automatically. "When?"

"The first night I came to this house," she reminded him. "Don't you remember?" She turned over on her side toward him, pulling the robe around her like a blanket. "I'd had a nightmare and was afraid to go back to sleep again, and you played Chopin nocturnes until I did."

"Really?" With a shrug that was meant to be indifferent but came out embarrassed, he began rolling down his sleeves. "I don't remember that."

"I do," Lauren said softly. "I'll always remember it." He looked over at her then, his face showing a muted surprise. "Won't you play for me again?"

"I don't play the piano anymore, Lauren," he said, his tone final.

"Why not?" she persisted. Reaching out impulsively, she grasped his arm to stop him from getting up and felt powerful muscles contract at her touch. "Why deny yourself the pleasure when you love music so much?"

"Because it's easier that way," he bit out harshly. "When you know you can't have something you want very much, you're better off cutting it out of your life

completely." Brushing her hand away, he got to his feet.
"You really should—"

"That's a terribly sad philosophy, Jason," Lauren
interrupted. "Sad and self-defeating." She met and held
his eyes with more courage than she knew she possessed. "Does that also apply to love?"

His dark gaze slid over her naked shoulders, down the
soft curves of her body outlined only too clearly by the
silky fabric. A sarcastic smile twisted his mouth. "Especially to love."

Turning abruptly, Jason started for the door. "It's
getting late. We both have to start getting ready for our
guests." Just before he stepped through the open doorway, he glanced over at her. The hard lines of his face
softened momentarily. "Good luck with the performance tonight."

She would need more than luck, Lauren realized as
she wrapped her arms around the pillow, hugging it
tightly. She would need all the courage that love could
give her. Her instincts told her that Jason wanted her as
much as she wanted him. Her skin was still burning
from his sensuous touch, and no amount of sarcasm
had been able to conceal the almost desperate hunger in
his eyes as they'd moved over her. But that wasn't love,
she reminded herself ruefully.

There had been a moment back there, as she gave
herself up to the hungry pull of his hands, when it no
longer mattered whether he loved her or not. The love
she felt for him would have been reason enough to give
herself to him utterly. Lauren was sure that Jason had
been aware of her feelings, and she reexperienced the
sensation of his strong thighs contracting against hers.
But he had pulled away from her. What if he reacted

that way after she played the sonata and exposed her feelings for him?

A wave of anxiety began spreading through Lauren, creeping under her skin like a cold, damp fog, wiping away all warmth. In spite of her fears, she was more determined than ever to play the sonata. Tossing the pillow to one side, she dragged herself off the bed. She had to find out, once and for all, whether Jason loved her. And she knew that he would never admit his love until he was totally sure of her. It would mean giving herself to him completely, holding back nothing. Jason was incapable of accepting anything less.

That realization would have frightened Lauren at one time. Now she smiled to herself as she stepped into the bathroom to ready her shower. She'd finally learned that Jason—if he chose to love—would do so just as completely.

But would he choose to love her?

Nine

———

As late as she was, Lauren stopped to take one last look at herself in the full-length mirror, trying to see herself as Jason might see her. What she saw amazed her. Her freshly washed platinum hair fell gleaming to her shoulders, her long bangs brushing the arch of her eyebrows, emphasizing the unusual flush suffusing her skin, the feverish glow in her pale-green eyes.

The opera-length strand of pearls she wore caught the light that shimmered over the silver lamé cocktail dress softly hugging every curve of her body. It was the most daring dress she'd ever worn. Its deep cowl neckline fell in soft folds, exposing the high slope of her breasts, and plunged halfway down her back. For a moment she had second thoughts about wearing it.

But only for a moment. She longed to be beautiful for Jason tonight. She wanted everything to be beautiful tonight.

Lauren spun on her heel and hurried out of her bedroom. It had taken her so long to get dressed that she hadn't been ready to greet Evan when he arrived. Annie, the housekeeper, had assured her that Clarissa was already downstairs, fiddling with the dining room arrangements, driving the cook crazy in the kitchen, and Jason was already stationed behind the bar in the living room, mixing cocktails for the arriving guests.

As Lauren went hurrying as quickly as she could in her high-heeled silver sandals down the hallway leading to the living room, she was surprised to hear the sound of loud voices spilling out the open doorway. One of the male voices was unmistakably Jason's.

". . . because you had no right," he finished with barely suppressed anger.

"I was under the illusion that this was my home, too," Evan's voice returned scornfully.

Good God, Lauren thought, they haven't been together for more than fifteen minutes, and they're fighting already. Well, she would soon put an end to that. Nothing and no one was going to spoil this evening—for Clarissa as well.

"All right, you two," she announced, sailing through the doorway. Her attention was immediately caught by the sight of Jason and Evan standing just a few feet away from the door, looking as though they were going to square off any second. "The referee is here now, and the fight is off."

"Lauren!" Evan cried when he turned to face her. "You look fantastic."

Lauren laughed self-consciously as she moved over to him. "So do you." She managed to slant Jason a glance. She'd caught the stunned look on his face when his dark gaze had first moved over her body, but his

eyes were expressionless now, the lines of his face taut
with anger. As she returned Evan's hug, Lauren wondered whether Jason was displeased with her outfit or
over the argument he'd been having with Evan.

"There's to be no more fighting," Lauren said, stepping out of Evan's embrace. "You don't know how
much Clarissa has been looking forward to this weekend, and I'm not going to let either one of you spoil it
for her." She kept her tone light, but determination
gleamed in her eyes as she looked from one half brother
to the other. "For the rest of this weekend, we're all
going to forget our past differences, and we're going to
be the most loving of families."

"I'm all for that," a familiar voice called out from
across the room.

Lauren had been so involved with Jason and Evan,
she hadn't noticed the man pouring himself a drink at
the bar. She gasped when she looked. "Carter!"

Her ex-husband sent her one of his most dazzling
smiles. "Hi, Lauren."

She stared dumbly at him for a moment, too outraged to speak. Though she couldn't see Jason, she
could feel the intensity with which he was studying her
reaction. The petite, dark-haired woman sitting in a
corner of the sofa in front of the fireplace, whom Lauren hadn't noticed until then, either, smiled quietly.

"What are you doing here, Carter?" Lauren finally
managed to get out.

"He's here at my invitation," said Evan with a
pointed glance at Jason. "I'd assumed it was okay to
invite my best friend to spend the weekend."

"Evan, you had no right," Lauren protested, echo-
ing Jason's words without realizing it. "How could you
do such a thing without asking me?"

"Because when I spoke to you on the phone, I didn't know things were going to turn out this way," he said, sounding as if he couldn't understand what she was making such a fuss about. "And then last Wednesday when I was playing squash with Carter—Carter and I always play squash on Wednesdays," he informed everyone else in the room "—I just happened to mention to him that I was coming out this weekend and that you'd be here."

"I'd been meaning to come down to the Cape one of these weekends anyway, to open up the house for the summer," Carter continued, casually crossing the living room, martini in hand. He came to a halt beside Evan and they exchanged a bewildered look; they seemed genuinely hurt that their motives had been so grossly misunderstood.

"Why, did I do something wrong?" Evan smiled ever so innocently. "I really thought you'd be pleased to see ol' Carter here, Lauren." With an affectionate laugh, he gave "ol' Carter" a pat on the back. "I know he's been dying to see you."

"I've tried to get in touch with you any number of times, angel," Carter added, smoothly picking up the conversation while Evan concentrated on his drink. "I've been wanting to talk to you."

It occurred to Lauren that they were like a vaudeville team executing a skit they'd performed countless times, only she was the one who felt like the clown. She'd never realized how alike they were. If a total stranger were to come into the room, he was sure to assume that it was Carter and Evan who were the half brothers.

They both had blond hair, although Carter's was wavy instead of straight and always managed to tumble appealingly onto his forehead, and his eyes were a light shade of blue instead of the startlingly deep-blue of Evan's. They both had features that were almost absurdly perfect, but where Evan's were sharp and fine, Carter's were softer, almost boyish. When he smiled, as he was doing now, the most adorable dimples appeared beside Carter's chiseled but slightly pouty lips, adding to his boyish appeal.

"If you really don't want me here, Lauren," he said, his tone sad but resigned, "I'll leave."

Lauren almost sighed out loud with relief. "Yes, I'd like you to leave."

"Come on, angel." He smiled disarmingly. "You know you don't really mean that." He ran his finger playfully up her bare arm.

"Lauren just asked you to leave, Carter," said Jason, his voice dangerous.

"Stay out of it, Jason," Evan said, stepping in. "This is between Lauren and Carter."

"It's not my choice, or yours, or Carter's," Jason shot back. "It's Lauren's choice." He looked over at her, his eyes hard, almost challenging. "Well?"

"But I've already—"

"What's the matter, Jason?" Evan cut her off tauntingly. "Are you afraid he's going to take her away from you again?"

Jason's hands clenched into fists, and every muscle in his powerful body stiffened. For an instant Lauren was sure he was going to hit Evan. The petite, dark-haired woman must have had the same thought because she sat up on the edge of the sofa, looking alarmed. Instead, Jason stepped back from Evan with an indifferent shrug. "Lauren is perfectly free to go anywhere she wants with anyone she wants."

"That's enough, both of you!" Lauren cried angrily. She resented their talking about her that way, not giving her the chance to have her own say. "Carter, I want you to—"

"Laurie, there you are," Clarissa called out gaily as she bustled into the room. "Oh, my, how lovely you look." Her smile turned coquettish. "Doesn't she look lovely, Carter?"

"She's never looked lovelier," Carter agreed seductively.

Turning away abruptly, Jason walked over to the bar with long, angry strides.

I've had nightmares like this, Lauren thought miserably, her hopes for a lovely evening disintegrating around her.

"Did Evan tell you about his other surprise?" Clarissa asked enthusiastically.

"There's another surprise?" Lauren stared at Evan blankly. She didn't see how he could possibly top the first one.

"That's right," Evan said as if it had slipped his mind completely. "Lauren, I'd like you to meet my wife, Monica." With a lazy sweep of the hand holding his drink, he indicated the woman on the sofa.

Lauren would never have believed that Evan could succeed in surprising her again, but he did. Knowing his obsession with beautiful young girls—he'd always claimed that a woman was over the hill at twenty-five—his choice of a wife was surprising, to say the least.

The woman Lauren hurried to welcome was in her mid-forties, almost fifteen years older than Evan, and plain to the point of being drab. She made no attempt to appear more attractive; her mousy brown hair was wash-and-blow-dry casual, and she wore no makeup.

Since everyone was wearing evening clothes, her navy-blue dress was too tailored for the occasion and without a hint of style. Yet behind the mascaraless brown eyes looking up at Lauren was a sharp intelligence and quiet, but considerable, strength. And that was another reason Lauren was amazed by Evan's choice of a wife.

Unfortunately, Lauren was ûnable to conceal her amazement, and she was sure Monica had seen it. Quickly trying to cover up, she offered Monica her hand. "This really is a surprise. I didn't know that Evan was married."

Monica returned her handshake. "Yes, most people are surprised." Her tone made it clear she was aware of the reason. The polite but resigned smile that followed implied it was a reaction she was used to.

"I hope you'll be very happy," Lauren added sincerely.

"Thank you." A warm smile softened her uneven features, and she sent her handsome young husband an unashamedly adoring look.

"Priscilla should be here any minute," Clarissa announced as she joined them by the sofa. "That woman will be late for her own funeral." She laughed girlishly and sat down next to Monica.

Lauren was relieved to see that at least her aunt's evening hadn't been spoiled. In fact Clarissa seemed to be thoroughly enjoying taking charge as she used to. "Come on over here next to me, Evan," she ordered gaily, patting a place for him on the sofa beside her. "Laurie, I think Carter needs another drink."

Carter, who'd been hovering by Lauren's side, sent Clarissa a grateful smile that became patently seductive when he turned it on Lauren. "I *would* like another drink." He held his glass out to her.

"Well, there's a bar two blocks from here," she informed him acidly, keeping her voice low so Clarissa wouldn't hear. Sweeping past him, she started toward the hand-carved Victorian bar where Jason was mixing another batch of drinks. Carter was about to come after her, but thought better of it.

"Could I please have a drink, Jason?" Lauren asked when she stopped by his side.

"Of course," he replied politely without looking at her; she might have been just another guest, a total stranger. "What would you like?"

"You're not angry at *me* are you?" Lauren demanded incredulously. "This wasn't my idea."

"Of course not." With a long glass rod, he began carefully stirring the vodka, vermouth and ice cubes in the crystal cocktail pitcher. "I see your husband—"

"*Ex*-husband," she reminded him sharply.

"—is as unconventional as ever."

"Jason, *I* didn't ask Carter here, and I don't want him here," Lauren explained. "I tried to get him to leave, but I can't risk a scene with Clarissa in the room."

"No, of course you can't," he drawled sardonically. "What would you like to drink?"

Her nerves stretched to the breaking point, Lauren sighed raggedly. "Are those martinis? I'll have one of those."

"A martini?" Jason finally looked over at her, but it was with a harsh frown. "I've never known you to drink hard liquor."

"I've never had a night like this, either."

"And it's not over yet," he muttered cryptically. With sure, deft movements, his beautiful hands poured some of the clear liquid into two cocktail glasses, then dropped a lemon twist in each one. He hesitated as he was about to hand her one of the martinis. "You really think this is going to help?"

"It's certainly worth the try."

He handed her the glass. "So he still bothers you that much?"

"His being here bothers me because this evening means a great deal to me." She looked up into his eyes. "I just don't want him to ruin our evening."

"He's already done that," Jason said with a twisted smile. Picking up his drink, he walked away from her.

Lauren's hands were shaking when she sat down at the piano. She didn't know how she'd managed to get through dinner. To accommodate the unexpected guests, Clarissa had changed the seating arrangement, placing Evan between herself and Monica, and Lauren between Carter and Jason. Having to deal with Carter's slick charm on one side and Jason's cold, dark silences on the other had been enough to destroy Lauren's appetite.

Everyone else seemed to be having a great time. Clarissa couldn't have been happier. Evan, with a constant stream of adoration from either side, was in seventh heaven. With Carter playing straight man, Evan dominated the conversation throughout dinner, telling risqué stories and spinning off wildly witty accounts of his recent business misadventures. Clarissa, Monica and Priscilla were clearly enchanted by the two of them. Lauren was not.

It amazed her that she'd once admired their outrageous sense of fun. She'd always hated being so shy and serious. All her life she'd longed to be like Evan and Carter, like her own parents—so glamorous and exciting, able to charm everyone in sight, never taking anything seriously. Now she recognized the immaturity and selfishness behind such behavior. She finally realized how easy it was to sweep into someone's life, spreading sunshine and happiness for a couple of hours or days before sweeping out again. Being there for someone day after day, through thick and thin—as Jason did—might not be glamorous but it was far more loving.

Lauren also found she deeply resented that Evan was getting the full prodigal-son-returns treatment while Jason was being totally ignored. She knew how it must have hurt Jason, and she made several attempts to start up a conversation with him, but he answered her in brusque monosyllables. Knowing that once he'd shut himself off behind that icy facade of his there was no reaching him, she finally gave up trying.

As upset as she was by the end of the dinner, Lauren was more determined than ever to play the sonata for Jason. She wanted to prove to him that there was someone who loved *him* to the exclusion of all others. But she still didn't know whether he wanted her love. She hoped she would soon find out.

Waiting for the rest of them to settle down with their after-dinner drinks, Lauren concentrated on relaxing the muscles in her arms and back. Through the triangle of space created by the raised piano lid, she quickly scanned the parlor, looking for Jason. He was sitting, all by himself, at the farthest end of the room.

"I think we're all ready now, Laurie," Clarissa called out from the love seat she was sharing with her friend, Priscilla.

Lauren nodded and turned her attention back to the piano. Taking a deep breath, she closed her eyes to block out reality and call up the emotion she would need to carry those first all-important notes. She found that the emotion already filled her being, was trembling at her fingertips.

As he always had, Jason held his breath while he waited for Lauren to gather together her thoughts and feelings before she began playing. He knew from experience how difficult the opening moments of a recital were for any pianist, and that Lauren was never more anxious than when she performed before people she knew personally. Suddenly she did something he'd never seen her do before: she opened her eyes and looked out at the audience.

Deliberately, Lauren's eyes met Jason's across the room and held them until she'd slowly lifted her hands high above the keyboard. Then, fingers taut with emotion, she swiftly dropped her hands to pound out the five powerful opening chords of the sonata. With intense feeling, she segued into the plaintively romantic theme.

Reassured that Lauren was in total control of her instrument, at the very peak of her form, Jason was finally able to relax in his chair. He was so proud of her, he found himself swallowing past a lump in his throat.

Lauren's fingers rippled effortlessly over the keys, making the lyrical but desperate love theme her own. It was *her* love for Jason she was pleading along with the music, *her* love that was begging to be heard. The imploring theme repeated itself over and over, growing in intensity. Unanswered, it turned back on itself. Frustration, despair and pain poured out of every note, growing until the anguish was overwhelming. As though unable to sustain such emotion, the first movement broke off abruptly with a violent, double-ripped chord.

Evoking memories of a lost love, a bittersweet lyricism suffused the second movement of the sonata, sweeping Lauren along with it. Longingly, her fingers spun out a promise of what that love might have been...what it still might be. The music grew dizzy with joy, wild with hope, and deeply sensuous.

Through the triangle of space beneath the piano lid, Jason continued to watch Lauren intently. On the surface, he appeared detached, but every note reverberated inside him, stirring up a longing as intense as the music's. Hunger began twisting through him when he saw the play of emotions on Lauren's face as the music poured out of her.

Her wide green eyes glowed feverishly, and her lips were parted, soft and moist. The light from the chandelier hanging over the piano turned her platinum hair into a halo, slid and shimmered over her silvery dress. Her revealing décolletage exposed exquisitely rounded curves, flesh as glowing as the pearls swaying over them as her body moved to the sensuous strains of the music.

Jason was enthralled by how totally Lauren gave herself up to the music, how completely she allowed it to possess her. He would have given anything to possess her as completely, to have her give herself up to him with such love and abandon.

Desire surged through him as he recalled the feeling of Lauren's mouth opening under his, the way her body had melted utterly against him. Until that night he'd never known a woman to open to him like that, nor had he ever wanted one to. And, although it had been hours, he could still feel the texture of her skin under his hands. He lifted one hand to his face and inhaled deeply. The fragrance of her body lotion still clung to his palm.

Jason's pulse jumped, and he recalled how Lauren's body had softened and changed in response to his touch. He had seen the desire darkening her eyes when she looked up at him, and he knew he could have taken her right there on the spot. But he'd waited too long for her and loved her too much to snatch a hurried moment before the guests arrived. A week wouldn't be time enough to make love to her the way he wanted to.

With the increasingly sensuous music swirling around him, Jason reaffirmed his vow to himself to do nothing that might wreck the new relationship he'd so carefully nurtured between them. Lauren was just beginning to trust him again. There were times when he thought she'd forgiven him for what he'd done to her that long-ago night. Not once during the evenings they'd spent talking had he seen that fearful look come into her eyes. Even though he warned himself against it, he was starting to hope she might be able to love him after all—but he hadn't counted on Carter showing up again.

The jealous rage and pain that gripped Jason every time he thought of Lauren with Carter began twisting in his guts. Deliberately he brought his attention back to the music.

Variations on the theme by Clara Wieck had been Robert Schumann's inspiration for the third movement of the sonata. Lauren had always played it as Clara's answer to Robert; now it became Lauren's declaration of love to Jason.

Slowly, achingly, her fingers drew out the deep sadness inherent in the music as she finally admitted to the emptiness and loneliness of her life during those last four years without him. As tentatively as the notes at first, she expressed her love for him. A desperate yearning that matched her own suffused the intensely romantic melody, becoming increasingly sensuous as the original love theme wound through it until the two themes were as deeply entwined as a pair of lovers in a passionate embrace.

The Clara Wieck variations had always been Jason's favorite movement in the sonata, but he'd never heard it played with such devastating emotion. Nor had he ever seen Lauren identify with a piece of music so totally. Suddenly he remembered how moved she'd been as a girl when he told her the story behind the sonata. "What a wonderful way to tell someone you love them," she'd said in her serious little voice. "Someday, when I grow up and fall in love, that's how I'm going to say I love you."

Jason sat bolt upright in his chair. Leaning forward, he studied Lauren carefully. Her face transfigured, her body taut with emotion, she was playing as though her life depended on it. A pulse began beating violently at the base of his throat. Had her choice of music been deliberate . . . or mere coincidence?

In the beat before she plunged into the wrenching opening of the last movement, Lauren wondered what Jason's reaction was going to be. Anxiety and frustration vied with a feverish hope as the love theme kept trying to break through the despairing chords that threatened to overpower it. But love could no longer be denied, whatever the outcome. Suppressed for too long, it came pouring out of her, a crescendo of passion, naked and unashamed, building to a shattering climax.

Lauren was shaking all over when her hands slid off the keyboard into her lap. In a daze, she looked over at Jason. It took a moment for the sound of enthusiastic clapping to break through to her, and she was vaguely amazed that there were other people in the room. Jason was not applauding; he seemed as unable to move as she was.

Before Lauren could get up, everyone came rushing over to her—everyone except Jason—and she found herself surrounded by smiles and compliments. Normally she would have been delighted, but tonight she cared only about one person's response, and she couldn't see it because they were all crowding around her. Lauren wished they would all go away so she could be alone with Jason, but she managed a vague smile and some polite thank-yous.

As Clarissa rattled on proudly, Lauren craned her neck, trying to see past her. Jason had gotten to his feet, but he was standing in the same spot across the room, one hand gripping the back of his chair. Why didn't he come over to her? Lauren wondered miserably. Hadn't he gotten her message, or was that his answer? A hand was being offered her to help her up, and she took it.

Jason stiffened as he watched Lauren allow Carter to help her to her feet. He was already irritated because Carter, who'd been sitting just a few feet away from the alcove, had rushed over to Lauren before anyone else had the chance to. When he saw the possessive smirk on Carter's face as he grabbed Lauren's arm, keeping her from following the others who were drifting back to their seats, he felt the beginnings of a dangerous rage.

Determined to keep his cool, Jason walked over to the side table where a large silver tray held a pot of coffee and several bottles of after-dinner liqueur. He was not going to fight Carter for Lauren again, he promised himself grimly.

Continuing to watch Lauren and Carter without seeming to, Jason poured himself a brandy. Since he was too far away to hear their conversation and Lauren's back was turned, he was forced to study Carter's face and guess from his reactions what Lauren was saying to him.

"Come on, Lauren, let's go someplace where we can be alone," Carter was saying with a suggestive smile. "We'll just talk, I promise."

"I told you, Carter, I have nothing to say to you."

"Then *I'll* do all the talking," he returned smoothly, tightening his hold on her arm as she sought to twist free of his grasp. "I've got plenty to say to you."

"If you don't let go of my arm, I'll kick you right in the shin."

Carter threw his head back and laughed loudly as though Lauren had made a joke. He knew she wouldn't dare make a scene in public. Lauren took a step back as though to take aim. He released her instantly. "I bet you would," he murmured, interest gleaming in his eyes; this was a new and exciting Lauren. He sent her a disarmingly dimpled smile. "How can you treat me like this when you know I'm still crazy about you?"

"Save the charm for someone else, Carter," Lauren replied wearily as she moved to get past him. "It doesn't work with me anymore."

"Come on, angel, you know deep down you still care." Carter fell easily into step with her as Lauren started toward the parlor, toward Jason.

Taking a long pull on his brandy, Jason watched them over the rim of his glass as they came toward him. He didn't realize that Evan and his wife had just come up behind him. He was too busy studying Carter, who was all easy charm and seductiveness as he continued his pursuit of Lauren. Lauren didn't appear to be paying attention to him, but her face was flushed with excitement, and her eyes gleamed with an almost feverish anticipation.

"They sure do make a gorgeous couple," Evan said when he saw the direction of Jason's glance, "don't they, Monica?" Reaching past Jason, he quickly refilled their glasses.

"Yes," Monica admitted wistfully. "They certainly do."

"I never saw two people who looked more like they were made for each other." With a wide grin, Evan handed one of the snifters back to his wife. "I'm glad they're going to get back together again."

"Are they?" Monica exclaimed.

Slowly, Evan swirled the brandy around in his snifter. "That's the real reason Carter came down here this weekend, to take Lauren back to New York with him."

Jason's hand tightened around his glass, and he knocked back almost half of his brandy. It burned like hell going down, just like the pain twisting his guts.

"How's it going?" Carter asked with a big, easy smile when he stopped beside them. "What are we going to do now?"

"I promised Monica I'd show her P'town," Evan announced loudly, catching the attention of Clarissa and her friend, who'd been deep in conversation on the love seat. "Why don't we drive over there and take in some of the night spots?"

"Oh, that would be lovely," Clarissa agreed.

Carter sent Lauren one of his seductive smiles. "How about it, Lauren?"

"I'd rather not," she replied. "It's been a very long day, and—"

"Come on, angel," Carter insisted possessively. "Sitting around here is such a bore. It'll be exciting."

"Oh, please, let's go, Laurie," Clarissa pleaded. "I haven't been out in such a long time."

"If you really want to." With a reluctant smile, she turned to Jason. She was secretly hoping that he wouldn't go so the two of them could finally be alone together. "Do you want to go, Jason?"

"No, not me," he said without looking at her. He knocked off the rest of his drink and set the glass on the table. "I have to catch an early flight to Boston tomorrow morning."

Lauren gasped. "Boston?"

"Well, we wouldn't want to keep you up too late, then," Evan said mockingly. "When you're almost forty, you need all the rest you can get. Right, old man?"

Jason shot Evan a look that wiped the smile right off his face. "Have a good time, everybody," he said evenly before he turned to walk out of the room.

"Don't worry, we will," Carter called after him.

Before she realized what she was doing, Lauren went rushing after Jason. She caught up with him just before he reached the door. "Jason, why are you going to Boston?"

He stopped and looked at her, but didn't answer.

"I mean, tomorrow's Sunday," she said, taking a step toward him. "Isn't the office closed?"

"I have some personal business to attend to," he informed her coolly.

Lauren stepped back. "Oh, I see."

"Will you still be here when I get back Monday morning?" he asked matter-of-factly. "Or were you planning on going back to New York with Evan and Carter?"

"I . . . I hadn't made any plans," Lauren murmured distractedly. That wasn't true. She had made plans; they were just the wrong ones.

"Well, if you do decide to go back on Monday," he requested politely as he pulled open the door, "please ask Priscilla to stay with Clarissa until I get back." Without waiting for her answer, he walked out, shutting the door behind him.

Ten

————

Peo...ple. Peo...ple who need peo...ple," sang "Barbra Streisand" plaintively, "are the luckiest peo...ple in the world...." A spontaneous burst of applause went up from the audience at the female impersonator's uncanny recreation of the famous star's voice and mannerisms.

Lauren did not applaud this time. She'd been trying to get into the spirit of things since the show started, a dozen impersonations ago, but she was no longer able to pretend she was having a good time like everyone else at the table. No matter how hard she fought it, all she could think of was Jason.

Taking another sip of white wine, she forced herself to concentrate on the performance. Every inflection, every gesture had been captured to perfection. The circle of light illuminating the stage narrowed, then went out dramatically as the song ended, plunging the entire nightclub into darkness. After a deafening round of applause, whistles and much foot stomping, the spotlight went on again, focusing on "Judy Garland," followed by "Diana Ross" and "Mae West." One by one, the other "stars" took their bows, and the waiters began moving from table to table to give everyone the last call for drinks.

"What do you want to do now?" asked Carter, deferring the choice to Evan as usual.

"I thought we'd take in another one of P'town's main attractions," Evan said as he motioned to their waiter for the check. "There's a bar just a couple of blocks from here that's supposed to be really something, even by P'town standards."

"What kind of a bar?" Clarissa asked, her cheeks flushed from more wine than she'd had in ages.

"A gay bar," Evan tossed off casually. In the shocked silence that followed, he exchanged a conniving look with Carter.

"That sounds fascinating," Monica exclaimed with more enthusiasm than Lauren believed she felt. The grateful look that lit up her plain face when her young husband sent her an approving smile was only too genuine.

"Yes," Clarissa was quick to agree, "that does sound...interesting." With a nervous laugh, she turned to her friend, whose mouth was still slack from surprise. "Doesn't that sound like it would be an interesting experience, Priscilla?"

"Oh, my...yes," said Priscilla, although she looked as if she'd just been invited on a guided tour of hell. "It certainly does." Like the other women, she obviously didn't dare be the one to go against Evan's wishes.

Lauren had no such problem. For Clarissa's sake, she'd gone along with Evan all evening, but now she'd had all she could take. "It's after one. I don't know about you, but I'm ready to call it a night." She got to her feet abruptly, sending her chair screeching over the sawdust-covered floor. "Clarissa, are you sure you wouldn't rather—"

"Come on, Lauren," Carter cut in. "We just want to have a little fun."

"Yeah, don't be such a little prude," Evan added, his voice full of contempt.

"I am not a prude, Evan." She turned on him angrily. "I would never presume to judge other people's life-styles, no matter how different they are from mine." Reaching over, she grabbed her beaded evening bag off the table. "I just don't get my kicks from using other people as entertainment, the way you do."

With a tiny gasp, Clarissa reached for her wineglass. Monica started brushing nonexistent crumbs off the tablecloth. Evan laughed sarcastically. "You know something, Lauren? You're getting to be as big a bore as Jason."

"And that's some bore," agreed Carter.

"You know something, Evan?" Lauren shot back. "I finally realized tonight why the two of you are always putting Jason down. It's because, deep inside, you're both jealous of him. You've been jealous of him all your life." Pulling her silver fox wrap from the back of her chair, she sent them each a slow, cool smile. "And you should be jealous because the two of you put together aren't half the man Jason is."

Lauren took a moment to enjoy the rage narrowing Evan's eyes before turning to her aunt. "I'm sorry,

Clarissa, but somebody's got to start telling the truth in this family."

"Oh, you're right, Laurie," Clarissa insisted with a desperate little smile. "Evan is just a big, overgrown boy. And I'm afraid he'll never grow up." Leaning against him, she reached up and ruffled his hair lovingly without noticing the murderous look he slanted her. "But that's why we all love him so."

"I think I'll take a taxi home," Lauren muttered. She spun around and quickly made for the exit. Before she reached it, Carter had caught up with her.

"Let's get out of here," he said as though leaving had been his idea. Smoothly he pulled the door open and held it for her.

"I'm not going anywhere with you, Carter," Lauren told him as she stopped in the doorway. "I'm going home."

"Okay," he agreed lightly. "So I'll drive you home."

"Thanks, but no thanks." She swept past him. "I'd rather take a taxi."

"It's off-season," he pointed out, following her outside. "Where are you going to get a taxi in P'town at this time of night?"

Lauren ignored him and, continuing over to the curb, peered up and down Provincetown's narrow main street. The full moon was at its apex, brightly illuminating the quaint shops, cafés and converted wharf buildings lining Commercial Street. At the height of the season, the colorful street would be teeming with summer people and tourists, and cars would be forced to negotiate it at a speed under ten miles per hour. Tonight it was as deserted as a ghost town.

"I'm parked just around the corner," Carter said.

A powerful gust of wind went up, knifing through the delicate fabric of Lauren's silver lamé dress. Quickly slipping her fur wrap around her, she continued peering up the street as if wishing could make a taxi materialize out of the fog beginning to sweep in off the harbor.

"Come on, Lauren," Carter insisted, impatience edging his tone. "We're both going to freeze to death out here." Grabbing on to her arm, he started tugging her toward the corner.

Lauren pulled her arm away. "No!"

"I'll just drive you home, I swear. All I want is a chance to talk to you," he pleaded with uncharacteristic seriousness. "You know, I've driven a pretty long way just to talk to you, angel. The least you can do is listen to me."

A fresh gust of wind went up, stronger than the first, whipping Lauren's hair around her face, stinging her cheeks. "All right," she agreed reluctantly. "But don't try anything, Carter."

"Why would I try anything?" he protested, sounding as if he were incapable of doing such a thing.

"Just see that you don't," she warned. Tugging her wrap tightly around her against another gust of bone-chilling wind, Lauren followed him quickly around the corner.

"This is it," Carter announced proudly as he stopped beside a fire-engine-red sports car. "What do you think of it?"

"It's very nice."

"Very nice?" A frown knotted his perfect features as he reached over to open the car door for her. Her response obviously hadn't been as enthusiastic as he'd anticipated. "It's a brand-new Porsche 944. It can do zero to sixty in eight-point-three seconds flat. Top speed is one hundred thirty miles per hour," he rattled on proudly as Lauren slid inside without his help. "Evan's been working on Monica to get him one just like it for his birthday." He laughed with satisfaction as he carelessly slammed the door.

"You're really something else, angel," Carter said when he'd slid behind the black leather-wrapped steering wheel. "Most women would give their eyeteeth to be seen in a car like this."

Lauren cringed inside at Carter's typically crass opinion of women. She was tempted to tell him that he shouldn't judge other people by himself, but nothing involving Carter mattered to her anymore. It amazed her that she'd ever cared for him at all. She stared out the side window, grateful that Truro was only a short distance from P'town.

Turning the key in the ignition, Carter slammed his foot down on the accelerator and revved the motor as loudly and enthusiastically as a teenager with his first jalopy. "But I should know by now that you're not like any woman I've ever known," he muttered, his tone managing to combine admiration with irritation as the Porsche zoomed away from the curb.

"I've really missed you, Lauren," said Carter, shifting smoothly into second gear. "More than I ever thought I could." He sent her one of his most disarming smiles. "I'm still in love with you, angel."

Lauren cringed again at her ex-husband's pet endearment, which she knew was a result of his having watched too many Humphrey Bogart movies. "You don't love me, Carter," she replied wearily. "I'm just the one that got away."

"Only because I let you get away. I'm not going to make that mistake this time." With supreme confidence, he executed the turn onto Route 6. "You know you still care about me. Why won't you admit it?" He slid his hand off the gearshift onto her thigh. "I was your first, angel. A woman never forgets her first."

"I had the measles once, too," Lauren returned lightly, brushing his hand away as if it were a mildly annoying insect. "But I got over it, and now I'm immune."

"What are you saying, that I'm a disease?"

"Something like that."

"Then you'd better watch out," he purred seductively. "Some diseases are chronic. They stay in your blood and you never get rid of them."

"That was before penicillin," she shot back.

"You're too much, angel." He laughed good-naturedly, refusing, as usual, to take her seriously. "Remember, *I* never wanted a divorce. And I still don't believe you did, either."

"Oh yes, I did!"

"No, you didn't," he protested with a dismissive shrug of his well-padded shoulders. "You were just mad at me because of that little fling I had, which had absolutely nothing to do with us."

"I thought it had everything to do with us."

"That's where you were wrong," he insisted, shifting gears automatically. "I never could get you to understand that a man is totally different from a woman." He slanted her an insufferably knowing look, and his tone was that of a professor trying to get through to a particularly dim-witted student. "You see, a man has certain urges every now and then, and he has to give in to them, if only to prove he's a man. Going to bed with those other girls was like...like having a soda when you're thirsty, that's all."

Lauren laughed and was delighted to find she could joke about something that had once caused her great pain. "You certainly had one hell of a thirst."

"I can't help it if I'm highly sexed," he murmured with a smile that managed to be both humble and smug. "But why couldn't you have been like Monica?" he added resentfully, as if the whole thing had been Lauren's fault. "Monica knows what Evan's like, but she lets him do his thing without giving him any hassles. She accepts the fact that the others don't mean anything as long as he always comes back to her."

"But I'm not like Monica, Carter," Lauren stated proudly. "And I have no intention of ever being like her. I think she's a very sad woman."

Carter shook his head, sending several curly blond locks tumbling attractively onto his forehead, and turned his full attention back to driving. He'd obviously given up on ever penetrating the denseness of her mind.

Lauren couldn't have been more relieved. She stared through the windshield at the moon slipping in and out of the trees, their bare branches swaying like long, skeletal fingers as the wind shook them relentlessly. Although Carter was driving very fast, she was able to pinpoint their location. The Caldwell house was less than a mile away.

Lauren couldn't wait to get home, even though she was sure Jason had already gone to bed. It saddened her that she wouldn't get the chance to see him again before he left for Boston in the morning.

"All right," said Carter unexpectedly, sounding somewhat exasperated. "If that's the only way I can get you to come back to me, I swear I won't screw around anymore, okay?''

"Oh, no," Lauren returned with a wry smile. "I couldn't let you make such a sacrifice on my account."

"Hell, it's not *that* much of a sacrifice," he allowed generously. "I'll tell you the truth, angel. I myself don't know why I did it sometimes." He looked over at her, confusion clouding his usually clear, untroubled eyes. "But it wasn't only my fault, you know," he was quick to add in his defense. "Women are always throwing themselves at me, and..." The sigh that escaped him was one of weary fatalism.

"And you feel compelled to catch them," Lauren finished helpfully. "Poor Carter. It must be quite a strain on you."

"Yeah," he agreed, her sarcasm going right over his curly blond head. "I admit it was fun at first, but I'm thirty-one years old, and lately..." He let out another tragic sigh.

"Lately there's not as much satisfaction in it for you."

"That's right," he exclaimed, clearly delighted that he'd finally gotten her to understand him. "It's like being on a merry-go-round that you can't get off."

He turned to face her, and for the first time, Lauren noticed the puffiness under his eyes, the beginnings of a slackness about his perfectly chiseled jaw. Unlike Jason's face, which was hard and lean and etched with lines from a difficult life that gave it character, Evan's face was turning flabby from self-indulgence. And where Jason's eyes held dark depths of emotion, Evan's clear blue eyes were like colored glass and just as lifeless, reflecting the emotional emptiness inside. Suddenly she felt sorry for him.

As if he'd sensed the change in her feelings, Carter smiled boyishly, giving her the full dimpled treatment. "I want to get off the merry-go-round, angel. And you're the only one who can help me do it."

"I'm sorry, Carter," Lauren said sincerely, "but it's too late for us. If you really want to change, I'm sure you'll find somebody else who—"

"But I don't want anybody else," he cut in like a petulant child. "I want you."

"It's not possible," she insisted. "I don't love you anymore."

"You *won't* love me, you mean!" He floored the accelerator and the Porsche zoomed forward, doing better than ninety miles per hour.

Lauren had to grab on to the edge of the bucket seat with both hands to steady herself. There were no streetlights along the narrow country road; the only illumination came from the car's headlights, which could barely slice through the dense fog rolling in off the moors. The moon had been swallowed up by the clouds, so Lauren couldn't make out the trees lining the steep embankment at the side of the road, but she could hear them as the sports car whizzed past, dangerously close.

"I'd like to get home in one piece, Carter," she said, working at keeping her voice calm and even. She felt sure it would only encourage him if he knew he'd succeeded in alarming her. "Do you have to drive so fast?"

"Yeah, I like driving fast. It's exciting." A perverse gleam animated his eyes, bringing his whole face to life. It suddenly occurred to her that the only time Carter felt truly alive was when he was doing something unconventional or forbidden. "You used to think it was fun once, too."

"That was before I grew up." Her fingers dug deep into the leather seat as the car shuddered around a hairpin curve; the blood drained from her face.

"You're not afraid, are you?" he taunted.

"No." She could barely get the word out, her mouth was so dry. "I just don't see why you have to take such risks. Is this another way of trying to prove that you're a man?"

"I don't have to prove a thing! It wasn't my fault that you were practically frigid," he shot back spitefully.

Lauren gasped as if he'd struck her. A violent gust of wind rattled the car windows and ripped the clouds overhead to shreds. The moon slid into view again, illuminating her pale face, the shock and pain widening her eyes.

He grinned with satisfaction when he saw that he'd finally succeeded in getting to her. Easing his foot off the gas pedal, he brought the speedometer back down to sixty. "I never had any trouble giving a woman satisfaction—ask any of them," he boasted defensively. "Maybe if you'd been better in bed, I wouldn't have had to go elsewhere to find *my* satisfaction, did you ever think of that?"

When had he allowed her to think otherwise? He'd always blamed her sexual inadequacy for his infidelities. But, somehow, hearing him accuse her of it now hurt Lauren more than it ever had. She wondered if men could automatically sense that lack in a woman. Maybe that was the reason Jason didn't want her.

Blinking back the tears that were welling behind her eyes, she managed a tense smile. "Then I would think you'd be glad to be rid of me."

"I should be, but I'm not." Swinging the car into the driveway leading to the house, he slammed his foot down on the brakes, bringing it to a screeching halt. "I don't know why, but you're still the only one who really turns me on." With one impatient motion, he shoved the gearshift to Park. It reminded her of the way he used to make love.

"There's just something about you, angel," he murmured with practiced seductiveness, "something untouchable." Sliding around in his seat, he leaned over to her. "Even when we were married, no matter how many times I had you, I never felt I ever possessed you." Smoothly he brought his face down to hers.

"That's because I never really loved you, Carter," Lauren said coldly just as he was about to kiss her.

He pulled his head back in surprise, but it took him only a moment to recover. "That's ridiculous."

"It's true," she insisted as he was about to move in on her again. "I wanted to love you. I really tried to. But I couldn't because I was in love with someone else... even though I didn't know it at the time."

He sat up and stared at her incredulously for a moment.

"And I'm still in love with him."

"Come on." He burst out laughing, obviously incapable of believing that she could possibly prefer another man to him. "Okay," he said as if he were willing to go along with her little joke. "Who are you in love with?"

"With Jason," she told him unhesitatingly.

"Jason? That old grouch? You've got to be kidding." He was about to laugh again when he saw the look in her eyes. It was a look he'd never seen before. A spiteful smile distorted the perfect line of his lips. "But he's got to be as big a bore in bed as you are."

"As a matter of fact, he's incredible in bed," Lauren returned defensively. "He's the best lover I've ever had." Pushing open the door, she slid quickly out of the car.

"Oh, yeah?" he spat at her. "Doesn't he mind that you're frigid?"

Lauren smiled. "I'm not frigid with him." She paused to enjoy the look on his face before slamming the door.

Tears burning behind her eyes, Lauren hurried up the long driveway to the house. Her high heels sinking into the loose gravel, she struggled against the wind that was whipping her hair around her face and stinging her skin. When she was close enough to make out the house through the fog, she looked up at the windows of Jason's bedroom, but they were as dark as the clouds being swept out to sea.

As she was about to slide the key into the lock, a tear slipped down Lauren's face, making her hesitate. As tired as she was, she suddenly dreaded facing the empty bed that was waiting for her, the promise of another long, lonely night.

Sinking down into one of the wicker chairs on the porch, she tucked her legs under her and, huddling in the fur wrap, finally gave in to the tears she'd been holding back all evening. Somewhere, an open casement window kept slamming against its frame under the relentless assault of the wind, drowning out her sobs.

Eleven

Jason was surprised to find the door to Lauren's rooms wide open. He could have sworn he'd heard a door being slammed shut—at least that's what the noise had sounded like from the living room—and he was sure it had come from that direction. "Looks like I'm losing it, huh, Killer?"

Killer's ears went up the instant he heard his name, then twitched nervously as they picked up the dark undertone in his master's voice. Killer's velvety black ears had done a lot of twitching in the last few hours, making Jason realize just how irrationally he was acting.

Lauren would have had to pass the living room to get to her quarters, he reminded himself. And he'd been sitting in there since everyone left, so there was no way he could have missed her if she'd come in. Unless she used the beach entrance at the back of the house, but that wasn't very likely at that time of year. It was far more likely, knowing Carter, that he'd managed to charm Lauren into spending the night at his place.

The knot of jealous rage that he'd been trying to dissolve with brandy for the last three hours twisted in Jason's guts.

In spite of his better judgment, he crossed the threshold and quickly scanned the brightly lit parlor. Half-empty coffee cups and brandy glasses, forgotten remnants of the party, lay scattered about on side tables and on top of the mantelpiece where the guests had abandoned them. The room was deserted.

Although he knew it was useless, Jason strode impatiently to the pocket doors and slid them apart with one motion. Moonlight streamed through the flowing lace panels on the windows, suffusing the bedroom with a pale, otherworldly glow, exposing every last empty corner. The sight of Lauren's paisley silk robe draped over the lacy bedspread sent still-fresh memories of that afternoon ripping through him.

Cursing himself under his breath, Jason turned to go back to the living room just as a powerful gust of wind slammed an open panel of the bay window against its frame. With a low growl, Killer lifted one of his front paws and stretching out his long, sleek nose, pointed in the direction of the noise while keeping well behind Jason's legs for protection.

"Some guard dog you are," Jason tossed over his shoulder disgustedly. Confident in the knowledge that his master was annoyed at something or someone other than himself, Killer merely disregarded his remark and followed cautiously behind him. Patiently, he waited while Jason stopped by the silver tray to pour himself a brandy before continuing over to the alcove, where the window panel was now creaking on its hinges in the diminished wind.

Setting the snifter on top of the piano, Jason secured the window, muffling the roar of the waves crashing against the shore, the wind lashing the beach grass. The pale, willowy strands streamed in the moonlight like soft, unbelievably fragrant platinum hair.

"Now I know I'm losing it," Jason muttered. Turning away from the window, he stepped over to the piano. Where the hell was she, anyway? Was she still with the group, taking in P'town's famous night spots— or had she gone off with Carter?

Sinking down onto the piano bench, Jason reached for his brandy and knocked back half of it in one gulp. He might as well have been drinking water; he couldn't even get drunk tonight, he thought. He rarely had more than two drinks and tonight he'd stopped counting at four. But instead of dulling his brain, the liquor made the stream of images he'd been trying to wipe out even more vivid; instead of numbing his senses, it sharpened them. He could feel each and every turn of the screw as the images of Lauren in bed with Carter kept unreeling in his mind.

Pain and rage exploded inside Jason, and he slammed his clenched fists down on the keyboard, over and over again, until the blaring dissonance finally shattered the unbearable images. Barely able to breathe from the constriction in his throat and chest, he tore off his black tie and ripped open the collar of his evening shirt. His dinner jacket was next; it barely cleared Killer's head when he sent it flying halfway across the alcove.

Resting his elbows on top of the piano, Jason buried his face in his hands. Traces of Lauren's body lotion still lingered on his skin. The same agonizing sense of loss he'd felt the night she ran away with Carter swept over him. He took a deep steadying breath, but that almost broke the solid lump in his throat into sobs. Sitting up, he began pounding out chords on the piano, unrelated chords at first, sheer noise, anything to fill the desolate silence and emptiness. Then, without consciously meaning to, he segued into the opening bars of his favorite Beethoven sonata.

The sound of music greeted Lauren in the hallway, quickening her footsteps. She was sure she hadn't left the stereo on, but obviously somebody had. She wondered who the pianist was. The phrasing was a bit rough but more than made up in power what it lacked in finesse.

She was still trying to place the aggressive, almost demonic style when she slowly closed the door behind her and continued into the parlor. She stopped short when she came around the corner of the L-shaped room and saw Jason pounding away at the piano as if possessed.

His eyes were closed, his face a reflection of the emotional intensity of Beethoven's *Appassionata*. As he played, the powerful muscles of his arms and shoulders rippled under his fitted silk shirt. His dinner jacket, for some reason lying on the floor at the foot of the piano, made a convenient pillow for a sleeping Killer.

Lauren's fingers went to her cheeks to make sure there were no telltale tears left. Other than that, she didn't move, afraid to break his concentration. Almost afraid to breathe, she watched Jason with a kind of wonder. Somehow she'd always known that he would play with such breathtaking power and intensity, but it amazed her to see the depth of emotion that was hidden behind that sardonic facade of his.

His beautiful hands glided expertly over the keyboard, building excitement with a rhythmic sweep of arpeggios. Suddenly he bent over close to the keys, making the repeated chords tremble. Goose bumps shivered up Lauren's arms; she was unaware of the sound she made at the back of her throat, but Killer's eyes opened and his head shot up when he heard it.

Bounding to his feet, the Doberman rushed to greet her, his backside wiggling ecstatically. Jason's hands froze in the middle of a crescendo.

"Don't stop," Lauren called to him.

Wordlessly, Jason watched as she hurried over to the alcove, her long platinum hair in tangles, her face flushed. He wondered whether her appearance was a result of the wind or from making love.

"Jason, it was beautiful," she said, her eyes glowing. "Please don't stop."

"I would have thought you'd had enough entertainment for one night," he drawled sardonically, closing the piano lid. "Back so soon?"

"Yes, I wasn't—"

"Or did you just come back here to get your things?" he asked coolly as he got to his feet. "I assume Carter's waiting for you outside in the car?"

Lauren stared at Jason uncomprehendingly. It was hard to believe that this was the same man who'd just been expressing his most intense emotions. Searching his face, she realized that he wasn't as cool as he pretended; emotion lingered deep in his eyes. Before she could decipher it, he turned his back on her.

"Why would you assume that?" she asked, trying to keep her voice steady.

"It seems to be common knowledge that he came down here this weekend with the express purpose of getting you to go back to him," he explained, bending over to pick up his dinner jacket from the floor. Shaking the jacket out, he slanted her a wry look. "And we all know how persuasive Carter's methods can be."

"I'm not responsible for Carter's actions, Jason, only my own." Lauren slipped out of her silver fox wrap and dropped it onto a chair with her purse. "And his methods of persuasion don't work with me anymore."

"Yes, I'd noticed that myself earlier this evening." A sarcastic smile pulled on the corners of his mouth as he slid on his jacket. "He didn't have to do a thing for you to encourage him to stay for the dinner party."

"I did not encourage him to stay," she protested. "It was only because of Clarissa that I allowed him to—"

"Allow, encourage," he broke in caustically. "When you come right down to it, it's the same damn thing."

Lauren was about to insist that it certainly was not the same damn thing, when suddenly she realized that, to Jason, it was. Jason hadn't changed after all. He still didn't love her, but he meant to see to it that no one else did, either.

"You're not my legal guardian anymore," she reminded him flatly. "Why should you care about Carter?"

Jason finished buttoning his jacket and shot the cuffs of his sleeves. "You're absolutely right. It's not my job to protect you any longer," he replied while managing to evade her question. "You're a grown woman now. And *you* should know better than anyone what kind of man Carter is." With one brush of his hand, he smoothed back the lock of dark hair that had fallen onto his forehead. The transition to legal guardian was complete. "If you decide to marry him again," he added contemptuously, "then the two of you obviously deserve each other."

"So we would have your blessing—such as it is—this time," Lauren shot back, refusing to show him how much his comment had hurt her. Bending over, she retrieved the black silk bow tie that was lying at her feet. She held it out to him with a brittle smile. "Does this mean that you'll give the bride away?"

The bow tie went flying out of her hand as a sudden uncontrollable rage shattered Jason's cool facade. Grabbing her by the arms, he shook her hard. "Don't play your sophisticated little games with me, Lauren, I'm warning you." His fingers tightened around her as if he meant to pull her over to him. For an instant Lauren was sure that he would, but he pushed her away instead. "Save the games for Carter, who taught you how to play them."

"My God, Jason, how can you be so blind?" she cried, any fear of rejection, all of her pride, forgotten. "Didn't you realize why I played the Schumann sonata tonight . . . who I played it for?"

He had started to walk away, but turned back to stare at her with dark, wary eyes. "I wasn't sure at first," he admitted. "Until I saw how eagerly Carter rose to the bait. And how you let him take it."

"What are you talking about? I didn't even know Carter was going to be here tonight!"

"Really?"

"You don't believe me," she murmured incredulously. "But why would I lie to you?"

He smiled harshly. "It certainly wouldn't be the first time. You've gotten together with Carter behind my back before."

"That wasn't how—"

"No? You dated him in secret. You ran away with him in secret. And you married him in secret." With each bitter accusation, he took a step toward her until he was so close she could barely breathe, let alone defend herself. "Well, didn't you?"

"You still haven't forgiven me for that," Lauren said slowly, somewhat dazedly, as the realization sliced through her like a knife. "I made a mistake, but I've been paying for it for the past four years. Isn't that enough?" She looked up at him as he stood towering over her, hoping to see some shred of understanding in his eyes. All she saw was the pain of betrayal.

Suddenly, Lauren understood the barrier she had always sensed between them, and she knew why Jason refused to show his real feelings for her. He did love her—though he would never admit it to her now. A sense of hopelessness swept over her. "You'll never forgive me for that, will you, Jason?"

The very real anguish in Lauren's voice took Jason completely by surprise. In another second she would have him believing anything. He wanted her so much, he was getting to the point where he didn't care if she *were* lying. Before he did something he knew he would regret, he turned and walked away from her. With a shaking hand, he picked up his brandy snifter from the piano.

"Won't you even try to understand?" she pleaded. "I was only twenty years old. I wanted someone to love me . . . someone who wanted my love." Pulling herself up proudly, she came toward him. "I'm not going to apologize for needing love, Jason, not even to you."

"But Carter didn't love you!"

"What did I know about love?" She laughed brokenly. "Who ever loved me? My parents, who I saw twice a year? The people who were paid to take care of me?" Stopping in front of him, she met his eyes directly. "You? All you've ever cared about was my talent."

"That's not true, Lauren," Jason said evenly. "That was what you always chose to believe."

"What else could I believe? Did you ever tell me that you loved me? Did you ever show me any—"

"I couldn't, dammit!" he ground out, slamming his glass down on the piano in frustration. "I—"

"Then how can you blame me for turning to Carter?" she broke in angrily, not giving him the chance finally to explain. "I was beginning to think that there was something wrong with me...that it was *my* fault that nobody loved me. And then when Carter, who could have practically any girl he wanted, started pursuing me, I was overwhelmed. He made me feel wanted and desirable and—"

"Yes, I know all about it," Jason cut her off savagely. His emotions had already slipped out of his control, and the thought of Lauren with Carter would have pushed him over the edge. He was glad now that she'd stopped him from telling her the truth. He just would have made a complete fool of himself. But he was afraid of what he might do if the jealous rage twisting inside him got the better of him. He started to walk away from her but she came after him.

"Jason, I was just trying to explain why—"

"You don't have to justify your attraction to Carter, Lauren," he cut in caustically. "I'm not going to try to stop you this time."

"Not even if I want you to stop me?" Lauren blurted out, stepping in front of Jason to keep him from walking out of the room. She didn't know where she got the courage. She knew only that she couldn't bear to lose him again. Impulsively, a bit desperately, she threw her arms around his neck. "I *want* you to stop me, Jason."

Jason stiffened at Lauren's unexpected embrace, and when her body brushed against his, he felt his control about to snap. "Don't!" His hands shot up to grip her wrists and break her hold on him. Pulling her slender arms from around his neck, he pushed her away, but he never released her wrists. Her head snapped back from the impact, sending her silvery hair swirling around her face. With a gasp of surprise, her lips parted, soft and unbearably sensous. And suddenly Jason didn't give a damn about the consequences.

"Are you sure it's me you want?" he bit out just before he pulled her against him again and his mouth came down hard on hers.

Lauren cried out under the bruising impact of Jason's kiss, but she didn't pull back. Somehow she knew that he wasn't angry at her but at himself for being unable to resist her any longer. Her mouth opened under his. A groan tore out of him, and he thrust his tongue deep inside her as if starved for the taste of her. His fingers tightened around her wrists and, wrapping her arms around the small of his back, he held them there.

She didn't need any encouragement to hold him tight; her arms clung to him eagerly. And she welcomed the deep possessive thrusts of his tongue as she returned his kiss with a hunger that matched his and stunned them both. Releasing her wrists, his long supple fingers slipped between hers, entwining with them erotically as his tongue slid sensually over hers. Her moan, mingled need and pleasure, was swallowed by his mouth as her body surged passionately against him. Without losing any of its intensity, his kiss gentled, became achingly tender, shivered through her.

A surge of the most intense love went through Jason when he felt Lauren's body melt utterly against his. But he'd wanted her for so long, had almost given up on ever having her, that he was afraid to believe it was actually happening. Tearing his mouth away, he searched her face intently. A tiny sigh of regret escaped her, and her eyes fluttered open reluctantly. They were silvery green, dazed with passion, and her lips were trembling.

He wanted to warn her that if they didn't stop now, he would be unable to stop at all. He meant to ask her if she wanted him as much as he wanted her, but he wanted her so much he didn't know what he would do if she said no.

As if she'd read the question in his eyes, Lauren smiled up at him. "Yes," she breathed. Her mouth, still wet from his, remained parted invitingly.

Jason felt a rush of joy go through him, so powerful it was close to pain. Sinking both hands into her silvery hair, he drew her face back to his. "You're so delicious, I could die for the taste of you," he murmured thickly before his mouth took hers again.

Lauren moaned when she felt Jason's tongue trace the outline of her lips before sliding inside to taste her with long, slow, thorough strokes. Sure of her now, he seemed determined to take his time, to discover and claim every inch of her mouth. Her arms went up to circle his neck. Trembling, she clung to him, letting him have his fill of her, but it seemed as if he couldn't get enough. He kissed her over and over again, deep devouring kisses, until they were both breathless.

Gasping for air, Lauren tried to drag her mouth away, but Jason wouldn't let her go. His teeth closed on her bottom lip, drawing it into his mouth. Dizzy with sensations she'd known only once in her life, she clung to him with every part of her.

Suddenly, never taking his mouth from hers, Jason bent his knees and swept her up effortlessly into his arms. He swallowed her gasp of surprise, and when her eyes flew open, he was watching her intently. Never taking his eyes off hers, he continued taking erotic little bites of her mouth while he carried her slowly into the bedroom.

Stopping by the side of the bed, Jason set Lauren back on her feet, sliding her body down his so she could feel his need for her tautening his every muscle, burning hot and hard in him. The shudder that convulsed her when she felt him made it almost impossible for Jason to restrain himself. One part of him wanted to tear off her clothes and throw her down on the bed so he could sink himself deep inside her. But the other part of him would be satisfied with nothing less than touching and tasting every inch of her until he felt her come apart in his arms.

Stepping back, he sank down onto the edge of the bed. Released unexpectedly from the strong support of his arms, Lauren swayed unsteadily. She seemed dazed from sensations she wasn't accustomed to, didn't quite know how to handle. "Jason?" she whispered, her eyes wide, her tone eager but a bit fearful, as though she'd never made love before and wasn't sure what he wanted of her.

"Come here," he ordered thickly. "Come here to me." Before Lauren could move, he reached out and grabbed her by the waist, pulling her between his parted thighs. She lowered her head to breathe deeply of his dark hair, and he lay his cheek against her chest. She shivered as she felt his ragged breath brushing the exposed tops of her breasts. Swiftly, he moved to fill his hands with her. When she felt his burning touch through the delicate fabric of her dress, her breath caught in her throat; it rushed out of her when she felt the moist heat of his mouth on her skin.

"Oh, yes," he groaned as he covered the slopes of her breasts with hungry little kisses. Her breath quickened, making the pearls shudder against her skin as he pushed the deep cowl neckline down even further with his mouth in his attempt to reach more and more of her. Tightening around them, his hands pressed her breasts together and his tongue slipped between them, thick and hard, sliding in and out until she was shaking uncontrollably and had to grab his shoulders to steady herself.

The silkiness and fragrance of Lauren's skin, the unbelievably sweet taste of her, were driving Jason to a point beyond control. His hands shot around her back to find the zipper of her dress and strip her of the last barrier between them. In his eagerness, he was rougher than he'd meant to be, and the zipper came apart in his hands. The silver lamé dress slid down her body, shimmering like the moonlight that flooded the room. With her platinum hair framing her ethereal face, with her long delicate body and incredibly pale skin, she could have been a moonbeam shuddering in his arms. He was blinded by her radiance, blind to anything but her.

Lauren's hands tangled in Jason's hair as his tongue traced the lacy scallops of her strapless bra while his fingers searched the back for hooks that weren't there. His teeth found the single closing in front and tugged it open. The scrap of ivory lace floated down to the floor.

"God, but you're lovely," he murmured, his voice ragged as he drank in the sight of her. "Even lovelier than I'd imagined and I've imagined this moment thousands of times."

Lauren was deeply shaken by Jason's startling confession, and by the achingly tender but tentative way he caressed her, as though he still couldn't believe that she was real, his for the taking. Her fingers tightened in his hair, tilting his face up to hers. "I've wanted you, too...for so long," she admitted, looking deep into his eyes. "I think I wanted you for years before I even realized it."

"You wanted me?" he murmured incredulously.

"It was always you, Jason." With trembling fingers, she traced the rugged outline of his face. "I've never loved anyone but you."

With a broken cry, he wrapped his arms around her, pulling her down into his lap. Lauren thought that she glimpsed tears in Jason's eyes just before he bent his head and took her mouth, blocking everything out. Denied for too long, the rush of love that went through her stunned her with its force and was met with an equal intensity as his kiss deepened, became deeply loving, filling her with a happiness she'd never known.

Aching for the feel of him, Lauren's hands slid between them to push his jacket aside and fumble open the studs on his shirt. Excitement made her fingers tingle when powerful chest muscles tautened under them, and she burrowed her hands into the rough silk of his hair. He bit the corner of her mouth, as if reluctant to let go of her, just before he released her abruptly.

Sitting back, Jason tugged his shirt and jacket off in one piece. Flinging them aside, he pulled her back into his arms, crushing her soft breasts against the hard wall of his chest. Lauren cried out as she felt his heated flesh straining against hers, and she threw her arms around him, clinging tightly to him. Bending his head, he drank, the pulse beating violently in her throat. They held on to one another for an endless moment, shaking in each other's arms; then the world tilted crazily around Lauren as Jason swung her off him onto the bed.

Twisting around, Jason reached over and slipped Lauren's silver evening sandals off, dropping a kiss on each instep as he did. His long, sensitive hands closed around her ankles, then glided up her legs in a shivery caress. Hooking the waistband of her panty hose, he peeled them down slowly. His gaze was another kind of caress, dark and possessive, as it moved over her body, lingering on the only part of her that was still hidden from him.

Hungrily he bent his head to cover the scalloped triangle of her panties with tiny nips and kisses. Lauren's breath caught at the unknown intimacy, then sighed out of her as she felt the heat of his mouth seeping through the transparent lace, melting her. His hands were shaking now as they gripped the edge of her panties, too impatient to be able to pull them off her delicately.

His dark, hungry gaze never left her as Jason bounded to his feet and tore out of the rest of his clothes, dropping them carelessly on the floor. Eager for the long-awaited sight of him, Lauren watched Jason just as intensely.

Shafts of moonlight poured down over his body, highlighting every gleaming muscle in his shoulders and torso, his long, powerful legs. Anticipation tightened inside Lauren when he stood naked before her; she physically ached for the feel of him. She'd never known such sexual longing. But just as he stepped over to the bed, a sudden anxiety gripped her. Carter's earlier taunts about her sexual inadequacy had come back to haunt her with a vengeance.

Jason saw Lauren's body stiffen; with a sinking feeling he recognized the fearful look clouding her eyes. About to lie down on the bed next to her, he hesitated. "What's wrong?"

It amazed her the way he could see right through her. "Nothing, I..." she was unable to continue. Helplessly she watched the rugged lines of his face harden defensively, his eyes darken with pain.

"I thought you wanted me."

"Oh, I do," Lauren cried. "It's not you, it's me. I..." she turned her face away, too ashamed to look at him. "I don't want to disappoint you. I...I'm not very good at this."

"What?" His laugh was part relief, part astonishment. "Are you kidding?" When he realized she wasn't, he sank down onto the bed next to her. "Christ, Lauren, I've been on the verge of exploding for the last half hour just from kissing you. No other woman has ever done that to me."

Reaching over, he slid his hand into her pale hair, turning her face back to his. "Where the hell did you get that idea?" He searched her misty eyes and found the answer before she could voice it. "That idiot, Carter? Did he tell you that?"

"Yes, because... I've never been any good at it."

"Well, you are now!" he bit out fiercely. As if to prove it to her, his hand slid down the length of her body, closing over the most intimate part of her. Slipping through the pale, silky hair his fingers opened her up, sliding easily inside. "You're burning," he whispered, his voice tender and triumphant at the same time. "Don't you feel how you're burning for me?"

"Yes," she gasped, her hips arching against the deep, searching thrusts of his fingers.

"And I've barely started making love to you." His eyes held the same fierce promise; his mouth kept it as he claimed her totally. Lauren's head snapped back against the pillow, and she cried out as he made her his in a way she'd never known, his mouth moving on her with hunger and need, a wild adoration.

The intense pleasure he took in her body amazed her, adding to her own. Circles of pleasure radiated from the very core of her, sharp and strong, tightening almost unbearably as they rippled through her. Making tiny, incoherent sounds at the back of her throat, she buried her hands in his hair, giving herself up to him. He groaned, and his tongue flicked liquid fire over her, quenching it and relighting it, over and over again until she was twisting beneath him uncontrollably.

Moving up her body with one powerful motion, Jason positioned his arms on either side of her, resting his weight on his elbows, leaving his hands free to caress her breasts. Parting her thighs with one knee, he slipped between them, pressing himself close to the liquid heat of her. Her back arched wildly, her nails digging into his shoulders when she felt the velvety hardness of him sliding up against her. Bending his head, he caught the swollen tip of her breast and sucked it into the moist heat of his mouth, his swirling tongue shattering her with pleasure.

Violently, Lauren dug her fingers into Jason's shoulders to pull him up to her and make him part of her. "Please..." she pleaded brokenly, "please...be inside me."

"I'm not through with you yet," he promised darkly, his warm breath brushing the aching tip of her other breast. His mouth closed over it, tugging on her hungrily while he continued sliding up against her with long, agonizingly slow strokes. The double assault on her senses sent dense, engulfing waves of heat washing over her. Loudly she cried out his name as if she were drowning and he the only one who could save her.

"Yes, now!" With one powerful thrust, he entered her, their bodies shuddering from the impact.

The extent of his possession stunned her, and her response to him was instantaneous and total. She no longer belonged to herself; she was lost in him as utterly as she once was able to lose herself only in her music. Caught up in the driving rhythm of his movements, she felt herself being swept away in a crescendo of passion she would never have believed possible.

It was all Jason could do to hold back. Never had he known such excitement, nor such a hunger to give as much as he took. He wanted it to go on forever. He couldn't get enough of the feel of her, the tremors that shook her and reverberated deep inside him, the wild little cries that tore out of her as she felt herself touched in a way she'd never been touched before.

He thrust deeper and deeper inside her, determined to leave his mark on her, to make it impossible for her ever to want or need another man. A fierce joy ripped through him when he felt her on the edge of ecstasy, all liquid fire shuddering convulsively around him, and still he held back. It was only when he felt her come apart in his arms that he finally let go, pouring himself into her.

Twelve

Are you all right?'' Jason asked, his breath still coming hard as he brushed a damp, tangled strand of hair off Lauren's face. Her heart was pounding violently against him, and he could feel her still quivering inside—a soft, warm, helpless fluttering all around him—but she hadn't moved or spoken during the long moments it took him to recover.

Lauren's eyes opened slowly, and she looked up at him somewhat dazedly. ''Yes, I'm fine. I—It's just that I've never...'' The flush of passion lingering on her face deepened, and when she was able to continue, her voice held a trace of wonder. ''That's never happened to me before.''

Jason had guessed as much from Lauren's reaction, but hearing her confirm it, seeing the truth of it naked on her face, moved him deeply. She smile up at him, her eyes shining. ''I'm so glad it was with you.'' The love he felt for her at that moment went so deep he could barely breathe. Unable to speak, all he could do was watch her smile fade, a sudden doubt dimming the light in her eyes. "You do believe me?"

"Yes!" he choked out. Sliding his hand into her hair, he brought her face to within a breath of his. "I've never felt anything like this, either, Lauren—ever." Softly, slowly, he brushed her lips with his. "But somehow I always knew it would be this way with you." His mouth closed on hers, and he kissed her with a tenderness that made her melt in his arms.

Regret, as sharp and sudden as a knife thrust, sliced through Lauren.

"Oh, Jason, why didn't you stop me four years ago?" she cried when she had dragged her mouth away. "You could have stopped me with one word." The unshed tears from four long, wasted years made her eyes gleam feverishly. "If I had thought there was even a chance that you loved me, I would never have married Carter."

"But I did love you. I've never loved anyone else," he said almost angrily, his hand tightening in her hair. "Did you ever see me with another woman? Did I ever so much as talk about another woman?" Releasing her abruptly, he separated himself from her, making her gasp from another kind of loss. "Why do you think I went crazy when you told me you were in love with Carter and wanted to marry him?"

Lauren stared up at Jason uncomprehendingly for a moment. "Because you were afraid he would ruin my career."

With a savage curse, he rolled off her and fell heavily onto his back. "I didn't care a thing about your career at that point."

"But that's what you told me," Lauren protested, the fine sheen of perspiration on her skin turning cold without Jason's body heat to warm it. "And you sounded so angry and bitter."

"How else should I have felt when you said your music didn't matter to you anymore?" he returned sharply. "And it wasn't because I only cared about your talent. That's what *you* always chose to believe."

"Why, then?"

Jason sighed heavily, as if he regretted his admission or found it too painful to discuss. "What's the point of going into it now?" His shrug was an attempt to dismiss the subject entirely. "You wouldn't understand." Sitting up abruptly, he turned away from her and swung his long legs over the edge of the bed. "You never have."

"But I want to understand." Sliding over to him, Lauren reached out and grasped Jason's arm. "Don't shut me out again, Jason, not now." Imploringly, her fingers dug into flesh still warm and damp from hers. "Talk to me, please. I want to understand."

Jason slanted Lauren a wary look over his shoulder. The taut lines of his rugged face softened instantly when he saw the pleading in her eyes. "Well, I knew how much you loved music...how you'd always dreamed of being a concert pianist," he got out with difficulty, "and I wanted to make that dream come true for you. At first, I think it was because I'd had the same dream, and I knew what it was like to have it destroyed. But later on..."

He turned his face away from her and stared down at the carpet for a long moment. "Later on, it was the only way I could show you how much I cared for you," he admitted, his voice thick with emotion. "Your music always meant so much to me because it was the one thing we shared completely. It was like a bond between us. And when you said you didn't care about it anymore..."

The tears that Lauren had refused to shed for four years suddenly flooded her eyes. "My God, Jason, you should have told me all of this that night."

He laughed sardonically. "Would it have mattered?"

"Of course it would have mattered! Why didn't you tell me?"

"I don't know." He turned to look at her finally, his eyes dark with pain and guilt. "Don't you think I've cursed myself a few thousand times for what I did to you that night? But you took me totally by surprise. I couldn't think straight. All I knew was that I'd lost you to Carter, and I went wild with jealousy. I wanted to hurt you the way you'd hurt me."

A tear slid down Lauren's face without her realizing it. "I never meant to hurt you. I never dreamed you cared enough about me that I could hurt you. If I had..." Fresh tears welled in her eyes and she found it impossible to go on.

"No, don't cry," Jason pleaded, her tears hurting him all over again. Quickly, he swung his legs back onto the bed. "It was all my fault." Reaching out, he caught her trembling face in his hands, what remained of his defenses crumbling. "I wanted to tell you how much I loved you, how much I've always loved you, but... I couldn't."

Lauren was stunned by Jason's confession. The hopelessness in his voice, the despair in his eyes sent a chill through her, freezing any more tears.

"I told you once, Lauren, being able to love comes easily to some people, but not to me. I don't have a talent for it."

Tears still sparkling on her lashes, Lauren laughed throatily. "Jason, how can you say that after the way you just made love to me?" Her arms went around him to hold him reassuringly. "I never knew a man could be so loving."

"That was because of *you*," he insisted with a soft, infinitely sad smile, "not me."

"That's not true!"

"Yes, it is." His hands released her face, and he slipped out of her arms, falling back against the pillows. "The only talent *I* have is for driving people away."

"Why do you say that?" she asked urgently, laying her head next to his.

"Because it's always been that way, ever since I was a kid," Jason said quietly as he stared blindly at the ceiling. "It never mattered how well I did in school, or that I always did what was expected of me; I always lacked that gift most children have of making people warm to them." As if to hold back the memories, to hide the painful emotions they evoked, Jason swung one arm over his face, hiding it from her. "But even then I was too proud to beg for love. So I learned to do without it."

Lauren felt her heart constrict at the utter futility in Jason's voice. Helpless, she watched a tiny muscle work in his jaw.

"I think I may have learned that lesson too well," he finished grimly.

Reaching out, Lauren took Jason's wrist and gently pulled his arm away from his face. "Nobody can do without love, Jason."

"I thought I could," he muttered under his breath. "For what it's worth, you're the only one I've ever let myself really care for, Lauren." An attempt at a self-mocking smile twisted his lips. "And even that was by accident."

Lauren's delicate arms circled his shoulders, drawing him down to her. Giving in to their loving pressure, he slid his body down, resting his head on her breasts. A sigh escaped him that was half a moan.

"What do you mean, an accident?" she prompted lightly, her arms closing around him.

"It's just that, I don't know why, my heart went out to you the first time I saw you." He let himself sink mindlessly into the irresistible softness of her. "You were such a sad, lonely little thing. So hungry for love and yet so proud. Somehow you touched something in me no one else ever had."

Enveloped by the fragrance of Lauren's skin, the comforting warmth of her embrace, Jason closed his eyes and let the memories wash over him. "I can still remember how that serious little face of yours would light up whenever I came home. You always seemed so happy to see me."

Jason's voice held a trace of wonder, as if he still found it difficult to believe, and it tugged at something deep inside Lauren. "I *was* happy to see you, Jason." Her arms tightened around him, soft and strong in a purely female way, fiercely protective. "I loved you."

"I know," he said, his voice raw, "in that totally unconditional way only children can love. No one had ever loved me like that." He buried his face between her breasts like a child seeking the most primal of contacts. "Before I realized it, you'd become very important to me, the most important thing in my life."

"Then what happened?" It tore out of her, the question she'd been dying to ask him for years. "Why did you stop loving me?"

Jason lifted his head and stared at Lauren in amazement. "I never stopped loving you."

"But your feelings for me changed," Lauren insisted. "Suddenly I couldn't reach you anymore. You were so cold and distant. And I was sure it was because of something I'd done ... because I'd let you down in some way."

"Is that what you thought? God, no!" He shook his head violently. "My feelings for you *did* change, but not in the way you think." Rolling onto his back, he pulled her on top of him, strong arms closing around her in a fierce hug. Her head fell onto his shoulder, her parted lips resting against the pulse in his throat. "I don't know if you remember the night of your first recital," he went on urgently, "when you were sixteen?"

"Yes, I remember," Lauren said, her voice barely audible.

"You were wearing a white gown. I'll never forget it. With layers and layers of ruffles. God, you were lovely. And instead of the usual pigtails," his hand glided up to her hair, "you wore your hair down, flowing over your bare shoulders." Slowly, as dreamy and hypnotic as the sound of his voice, his long, sensitive fingers stroked her hair. "Well, that was the first time I realized that the awkward young girl I'd known had turned into a very desirable young woman." His hand came to a sudden stop. "It was one hell of a surprise, let me tell you."

Jason drew a long, harsh breath, and Lauren felt it vibrate against her rib cage as he let it out in ragged pieces. Only then did she realize she was barely breathing.

"And then, in the dressing room later," he went on, his voice thick with the memory, "you threw yourself into my arms with your usual innocent abandon, and . . ." Searchingly his hand began to move down her back. "And I found that I was becoming aroused." His fingers dug into the rounded flesh of her hip, pressing her against him. "Aroused in a way I'd never been with any other woman." His hand went slack, then slid off her, falling onto the mattress with a dull thud. "Christ, I was shocked out of my mind."

"Why?" Lauren lifted her head and searched Jason's tortured face intently. "It wasn't as if we were related."

"But I was your legal guardian," he insisted. "I was sworn to protect you, not take advantage of your love and dependency."

"Oh, Jason." Lauren smiled softly, knowingly. "You could never take advantage of anyone."

With a harsh sigh, his head turned on the pillow. "I was afraid I wouldn't be able to trust myself because I wanted you so much. That's why I had to keep you at a safe distance until you came of age." He laughed suddenly, a single, bitter laugh. "Of course, by then I'd destroyed any chance I might have had with you. The ironic part is that I really believed I was doing the right thing."

Deeply moved, Lauren longed to say something reassuring to Jason, to reach out and touch him, but she was afraid to stop the flow of words that were finally pouring out of him. Having waited so long for those words, she desperately needed to hear them.

"But when I saw you withdrawing from me more and more, confused and hurt at first, then resentful," he went on, anguish grating in his voice, "I finally realized I'd made a terrible mistake. But it was too late. And the more you withdrew from me, the more hurt and sarcastic I became, until I made you stop loving me and I finally drove you away."

"Jason, you didn't drive me away. I ran away because I couldn't deal with the feelings you'd aroused in me, either." Grabbing on to his shoulders, Lauren slid up his body, to stare down into his face. "And I've never stopped loving you, not even when I wanted to...not even when I tried to with Carter." Smiling softly, she brought her face down to his. "I could never stop loving you. I know that now. You've been the center of my life for too long."

With a broken cry, his mouth reached up for hers, and he wrapped his arms around her, crushing her to him. Desperation mingled with love in his kiss, and she could feel him begin to stir against her—then the mattress started bumping up and down under them.

Pulling his mouth away, Jason muttered, "What the hell is that?"

Looking down, they saw Killer crawling out from under the bed, and they burst out laughing simultaneously. After a long, luxurious stretch, and a thorough body shake, he looked up at them, his clipped black ears at attention. He seemed to be reconsidering jumping onto the bed as he'd apparently intended.

Ever the sophisticate, Killer quickly evaluated the situation and sank down onto the pile of clothes they'd left strewn on the carpet in their eagerness. Stretching out comfortably, he crossed one long, elegant paw over the other and rested his head on them, closing his eyes nonchalantly. But his ears remained up like antennae, ready to pick up the slightest change in the situation.

"When did he go under the bed?" Lauren asked, still breathless from laughing—and from Jason's kiss.

"I have no idea," Jason returned wryly. "I was rather involved at the time."

"I'd forgotten all about him."

"It seems we managed to forget about everything and everybody, including the time," Jason pointed out, nodding in the direction of the windows. "Everyone must have come home hours ago."

Only then did Lauren notice the delicate hues of dawn spilling into the bedroom, suffusing it with a rosy light. Looking over her shoulder, she could see the moors in the distance, gleaming with dew, dotted with the first wild roses of spring.

"I think I'd better get going," Jason muttered with a reluctant sigh. Gripping her waist, he slid her off him.

"No, don't go!" She didn't want the night to end. There were still so many things she wanted to ask him, to tell him. "Why do you have to go?"

"Because everybody will be getting up soon," he explained, sitting up on the edge of the bed. "You don't want anyone to see me coming out of your bedroom at this hour of the morning, do you?"

For once, Jason's legal-guardian manner made Lauren smile. "Don't tell me you're trying to protect my reputation?"

One thick black eyebrow rose when he realized she was making fun of him. "I know it's an old-fashioned notion these days," he allowed dryly, bending over to pick up his briefs off the floor, "but yes, I am."

"Thanks for the try, but I'm afraid you're too late." Sliding over to him, she reached out, pulled the briefs out of his hand and dropped them on the floor. "I've already told Carter I'm in love with you. As a matter of fact, I told him that we're lovers."

"What?"

"I had to. It was the only way I could get rid of him. I didn't want him to go on thinking there was a chance I might go back to him." Sensing his hesitation, she searched his puzzled face. "You're not sorry I told him, are you?"

"No, of course not." Jason still found it difficult to believe that Lauren preferred him to Carter; he was sure that Carter had found that particular piece of news even more incredible. Slanting Lauren a bemused glance, he bent over to retrieve his briefs again. "I just wish I could have seen his face when you told him."

"It was worth seeing," Lauren admitted with a delighted laugh. Moving swiftly, she scooped up the briefs before Jason got the chance to. When he reached for them, she lifted them high above her head. "By now—knowing him—I'm sure he's already told everyone else." Waving the white triangle like a flag, she sent it sailing across the room. "So, you see, my reputation is already hopelessly lost."

Mischief gleaming in her eyes, Lauren went up on her knees and threw her arms lightly around Jason's neck. "Just what do you plan to do about it?" Playfully she dropped a kiss on the tip of his nose. "Are you going to make an honest woman of me or not?"

"What about your life in New York?" Jason asked evenly, evasively. "Wouldn't you miss the excitement?"

"About as much as I would miss the emptiness and the loneliness that went with it," she admitted with a rueful smile. She tossed her head theatrically, sending her pale hair swaying around her face. But it took more acting ability than Lauren ever knew she possessed to keep her voice light and carefree. "I know how you feel about marriage, Jason, so if you don't want to marry me, it's okay. I'll just have to be your mistress."

"But I *do* want to marry you," he got out with difficulty. "I've never wanted anything else, but . . ."

"But?"

His eyes met and held hers for a long moment. He looked like a man about to divulge a terrible secret from his past. Running a nervous hand through his hair, he finally muttered, "I'm sixteen years older than you."

Lauren laughed. "Tell me something I don't know."

Dropping his eyes somewhat guiltily, he grated, "I'm impossible to live with."

"I told you to tell me something I don't already know, Jason," Lauren teased warmly.

"I'm moody and irascible and—"

"That's right," she said, lowering her mouth to his, "talk me out of it." Softly she molded her lips to his. With the tip of her tongue she lovingly drank the moist warmth of him. A groan tore out of him, and he grabbed on to her. Just as the kiss was deepening, threatening to spill out of control, he dragged his mouth away.

"Don't you understand?" he bit out miserably, his eyes dark with anguish. "I love you, Lauren, but I don't know if I can make you happy. If I drove you away again—" His voice broke off; the pain that possibility caused him made it impossible for him to continue.

"But you *do* make me happy, Jason," Lauren cried. "The only time I was unhappy was when I thought you didn't love me anymore." She spilled across his lap. "Except for my music, the only time I feel alive is when I'm with you."

Happiness glowed in Lauren's eyes, naked and unafraid, as she looked up at him. Her face was radiant, blinding him. It amazed Jason that he could be the cause of so much happiness. Carefully, he gathered her up in his arms, like a promise he desperately longed to believe in.

A contented sigh escaped her as she snuggled up to him, fitting herself against him. Her cheek settled into the curve of his shoulder, her parted lips drinking the pulse that beat erratically at the base of his throat.

"Not being loved . . . being made to feel you're unlovable is a terrible thing to have to live with, Jason," Lauren murmured on his skin as her lips slowly moved up his throat, along the hard line of his jaw. "*I* know, because that's how I always felt before you took me in." Tenderly her lips continued trailing words and moist little kisses all over his face. "But once you realize that I love you *because* of the way you are," she paused to drag kisses over his burning eyelids, "I don't think you'll be impossible to live with at all."

Jason's arms tightened convulsively around Lauren, crushing her to him as if he meant to make her part of him. Once again he'd tried to do the right thing—to save her from himself—but he realized that he could no more do without her than he could live without the heartbeat pounding inside him, sending desire pulsing through his veins. This strange new image of himself he saw reflected in her eyes, as sure and strong as the love she had for him, made him almost able to hope again.

"Kiss me," he ordered fiercely as his mouth sought and found hers. Without hesitation, her mouth opened under his. Everything in her opened to him, and he felt an overwhelming tenderness for her melting into his blood. And suddenly Jason knew beyond the shadow of a doubt that happiness *was* possible—no one could ever love her as much as he did.

"Marry me, Lauren," he pleaded raggedly on her lips.

"Yes," she breathed. "Oh, yes."

Sinking both hands into her hair, he tilted her face back so he could see deep into her eyes. "There's one thing you can always be sure of," he vowed thickly. "I'll never love anyone else but you."

"I know," she said, her silvery hair sliding through his fingers like moonbeams. She laughed suddenly. "Except for the children, of course."

"The children?" he stammered.

"You're great with children, Jason. You should have some of your own." Softly her fingers went up to caress his cheek. "I know you'll be a wonderful father."

Her face blurred before him as tears suddenly filled his eyes. "Jason, what's wrong?" he heard her ask. "Don't you want children?"

"Yes, it's just that when I though I'd lost you," he explained brokenly, "I resigned myself to never getting married or ever having a family like most people." He made an attempt at a wry smile. "I guess I still can't believe this is happening."

A rush of love went through Lauren, so intense it took her breath away. She longed to show Jason how much she loved him, to assure him that he would never be without love again. Sliding off his lap, she stretched across the sheet, her naked body shimmering in the silvery light of dawn. "Jason, you once taught me to believe in myself. Let me teach you to believe in us." Her face radiant with love, she lifted her slender arms up to him.

Jason laughed softly. "It looks like the pupil has surpassed the master," he said as he let Lauren draw him into her arms.

Ears twitching, Killer's head went up. With a resigned sigh, he crawled back under the bed.

Silhouette Desire

COMING
NEXT MONTH

EYE OF THE TIGER—Diana Palmer
Eleanor had once loved Keegan—handsome, wealthy and to the
manor born. The differences between them were great, and time
hadn't changed them. But the passion was still there too.

DECEPTIONS—Annette Broadrick
Although Lisa and Drew were separated, the movie stars agreed
to make a film together. Would on-camera sparks rekindle
passionate flames off-camera as well?

HOT PROPERTIES—Suzanne Forster
Sunny and Gray were rival talk-show hosts, brought together in a
ratings ploy. Their on-air chemistry sent the numbers soaring—
but not as high as Sunny's heart!

LAST YEAR'S HUNK—Marie Nicole
Travis wanted to be known for his acting, not his biceps.
C. J. Parker could help him, but business and pleasure don't
always mix . . . and she had more than business in mind.

PENNIES IN THE FOUNTAIN—Robin Elliott
Why was Megan James involved with big-time crook
Frankie Bodeen? Detective Steel Danner had to know. He'd fallen
in love at first sight, and he was determined to prove
her innocence.

CHALLENGE THE FATES—Jo Ann Algermissen
Her child might be alive! Had Autumn and Luke been victims of
a cruel lie—and could they pick up the pieces and right the
wrongs of the past?

AVAILABLE THIS MONTH:

THE FIRE OF SPRING
Elizabeth Lowell

THE SANDCASTLE MAN
Nicole Monet

LOGICAL CHOICE
Amanda Lee

CONFESS TO APOLLO
Suzanne Carey

SPLIT IMAGES
Naomi Horton

UNFINISHED RHAPSODY
Gina Caimi

READERS' COMMENTS ON SILHOUETTE DESIRES

"Thank you for Silhouette Desires. They are the best thing that has happened to the bookshelves in a long time."
—V.W.*, Knoxville, TN

"Silhouette Desires—wonderful, fantastic—the best romance around."
—H.T.*, Margate, N.J.

"As a writer as well as a reader of romantic fiction, I found DESIREs most refreshingly realistic—and definitely as magical as the love captured on their pages."
—C.M.*, Silver Lake, N.Y.

"I just wanted to let you know how very much I enjoy your Silhouette Desire books. I read other romances, and I must say your books rate up at the top of the list."
—C.N.*, Anaheim, CA

"Desires are number one. I especially enjoy the endings because they just don't leave you with a kiss or embrace; they finish the story. Thank you for giving me such reading pleasure."
—M.S.*, Sandford, FL

*names available on request